Kadve P

(Bitter Discourses)

Teachings of the world-famous Revolutionary National Saint Jain Munishree Tarunsagar Ji

A unique collection of 'Golden Sutras' of 8 parts of much discussed book, 'Kadve Pravachan' by Munishree, delivered by him during his travelling & stay from 2004 to 2014 in Gujarat, Maharashtra, Karnataka, Chhattisgarh, M.P, Rajasthan, U.P. and Delhi.

Revolutionary National Saint
Jain Munishree Tarunsagar Ji

Publisher : **Diamond Pocket Books (P) Ltd.**
X-30, Okhla Industrial Area, Phase-II
New Delhi-110020

Phone : 011-40712100, 41611861
E-mail : sales@dpb.in
Website : www.dpb.in
Edition : 2016
Printed by : Adarsh Printers, Delhi- 110032

Translated by
V.A. Upadhye
Edited by
Ashok Kumar Sharma, PhD
Kadve Pravachan
By - *Munishree Tarunsagar Ji*

Introduction

Munishree Tarunsagar Ji will be remembered for many centuries

I heartily feel very honoured to present this volume, 'Kadve Pravachan' (Bitter Discoures) which is based on the thoughts of Revolutionary National Saint Jain Munishree Tarunsagar Ji.

How may one describe about Munishree?

Munishree Tarunsagar ji is a legendary Jain saint whose explosive proclamation to throw open the access to Bhagawan Mahaveer by bringing him out from the corridors and sanctum sanatorium of the temple created a commotion. How is he such a phenomenal saint that even the non-Jains throng to listen to his discourses and bestow on him the title of National Saint? He is such a legendary orator whose discourses can be scathing and fiery and at the same time act like a soothing balm and touch the inner chord of the devotees' hearts. He is a miraculous personality who attracts the masses, celebrities, politicians and artists alike or he is such a personality who has taken birth on this earth to be renowned worldwide in the Guinness Book of World Records and Limca Book of World Records. One has to spend one's entire lifetime in order to understand him and his contribution to mankind.

I had the honour to know Munishree during his journey when I was in Chhattisgarh as an author and a motivational speaker. By then, six of my bestselling books were already published in 12 languages and millions had participated in my seminars. Frankly speaking, I must admit that I had hardly visited any saint but there was something special about Munishree. I went to hear him during my Chhattisgarh journey and I was amazed to see the large stage, an audience of 25000 to 30000 people, and arrangement akin to being the guest to a political bigwig. I realized that this was no ordinary saint.

As soon as he started roaring from the stage, there was no sign of the applause getting a respite at any time. I found children, youth, senior veterans, Jain women, common people, the rich and the poor alike- everyone- applauding, at times restlessly introspecting and also greeting him with reverence. I returned with tremendous memories of the day.

After this, I had the privilege and good fortune of spending a lot of time with him. I spent some time with Munishree in the homes of the Chief Ministers of Chhattisgarh and Madhya Pradesh, Dr Raman Singh and Mr Shivraj Singh respectively. The closer I got to him, the more I was impressed with him. Since he was endowed with Deeksha at a young age, he could not acquire proper school education and yet he imparts such profound knowledge which can overshadow the degrees of many enlightened and highly qualified professors. I tell him very often that he is superior to many MBAs.

When he plans a strategy for any programme, his arrangements, style, capability of management and vision resemble preparations made by a CEO of any multi-national conglomerate. Munishree Tarunsagar Ji can never dream small. Whenever he takes up any project, it is bound to reach the pinnacle of success. The art of expressing profound knowledg

a few words creates a turmoil in the listener's mind, it is an
egral part of Munishree's persona.

His admirers have instituted the 'Tarun Kranti' award in
s name and I was given the responsibility of the National
esident for looking after its affairs. During the last four years,
has been awarded to prominent luminaries like Dr Kiran
edi, Baba Ramdev ji, Smt. Menaka Gandhi, Pranav Pandya ji,
amesh Chandra ji Aggarwal, Gulab Kothari ji, Virendra Hegde
Shantilal Mutha ji and many more. With the association of
ese notable personalities, the award has acquired exclusivity
f its own and made it coveted. In order to receive the award by
e Munishree himself, these luminaries presented themselves
various towns. It was a matter of great pride for us also to
cknowledge the contribution of such great people through this
ward.

I make it a point to remain alert whenever I accompany him.
Nobody can anticipate when an amazing and wonderful idea
would escape from his brilliant mind and lips. It is also a matter
of great and unique pleasure to be with him. His child-like
playfulness, deep insight and thoughtfulness, his views on social
development, assertive administration are truly a representation
of his multifaceted personality and it is interesting to watch
him expressing himself in these forms from time to time with
amazing unpredictability. He is very firm and assertive and if he
has made up his mind on some issue, nobody can stop him. This
is probably the reason that when he decides to do something,
he ensures that it is accomplished with the highest levels of
standards.

Some compare him with Kabir or with Aristotle while others
compare him with Osho and many others think that he is like
some other legends. I do not wish to compare him with anyone
else. I want that the coming generations in the future know

him as the Revolutionary Saint Tarunsagar Ji and nobody else. Each passing century has seen some great souls and they are remembered for many more centuries. Munishree Tarunsagar Ji belongs to our era and he is one of the great souls of our time.

This revolutionary book, 'Kadve Pravachan' (Bitter Discoures) by Munishree Tarunsagar Ji will be launched in fourteen languages in 2014 simultaneously on the same day and from the same platform. This moment will be recorded in the golden words in the history of Indian book publishing.

I would like to submit to the readers that every thought in this book is a scripture in itself. I would like the readers to read his thoughts very deeply and to assimilate them in their life thus carving a path of progress. Each of his thoughts has the power to change your life. It is my august desire that this book should help you to take you to the peak of success in every field of your life. With a million humble greetings to Munishree Tarunsagar Ji, I wind up here.

– Dr Ujjwal Patni
International Trainer and Motivational Speaker
Famous author of 'Safal Vakta-Safal Vyakti'
'Power Thinking', and 'Jeet ya Haar'
www.ujjwalpatni.com
training@ujjwalpatni.com

Preface

Munishree Tarunsagar Ji is a famous saint in Jain tradition. Munishree has been acknowledged for his work not only among Jains but also among the followers of other castes, creeds and religions. He is no ordinary saint; he is a revolutionary saint and a philosopher. Blind followership of traditions and faiths is not a part of his thought-process. He is igneous, and ignited like fire.

Today the society needs someone like Munishree Tarunsagar Ji to transform its outlook and profile, someone who would wash away its vices and cleanse it thoroughly.

Each verse in 'Kadve Pravachan' is as precious as a diamond. The 'Sutras' enumerated in 'Kadve Pravachan' are so scathing that they pierce through your thought-process. The verses written in light hearted and seemingly trivial manner are to, in fact, shatter the inconsistencies and deformed profile of the society. The thoughts are sharp and the language is as carefree as his personality. While we may call them 'Kadve Pravachan', I strongly believe that these are, in reality, deliciously sweet in content. It is very rare to find anywhere else the sweetness seen in Munishree's expressions. This is my personal impression. I have been serving him for past many years and he has blessed me with great compassion.

This is a unique second version of 'Kadve Pravachan' (Bitter Discourses). It has a compilation of discourses which he delivered last year during his tour and stay in various cities. The popularity of 'Kadve Pravachan' can be judged from the fact that it has been translated into many languages and read all over the country. While reading this book you must bear the fact in your mind that, medicine and truth are always scathing and bitter. It must be our endeavour that we must internalize Munishree's thoughts and spread them in every home.

With best wishes.

Ramesh Chandra Agarwal
Chairman,
Dainik Bhaskar Group

Wishes and Blessings

Shravana tradition is rich because it has given numerous saints like Acharya Pushpadant, Acharya Bhutbali, Acharya Kundakunda, Acharya Samantbhadra and many more who have influenced the world and who are spiritually endowed. These are recognised as the greatest thinkers in Jain tradition and Munishree Tarunsagar Ji has been striving hard to continue to keep this tradition alive to make it immortal.

No subject is a taboo for Munishree Tarunsagar Ji's introspection and study, be it ideal marital life, materialistic prosperity, administration of the nation, state administration for the welfare of the people, education and many more. He has been sugar coating all these complex and bitter topics with his wisdom, in-depth study and bringing them within the reach of the common people. He has proved himself to be an inspiration behind the transformation of our era and enlightenment of the common masses towards positivity. Tarunsagar Ji's capability is unparalleled in addressing the problems of contemporary generation and representing them.

In this world, when one explorer discovers the means of salvation, then everyone around him starts nurturing the aim of achieving it. A philosophical explorer possesses the light of knowledge, rays of which start illuminating innumerable people's life and this is the reason, this blissful light is reaching in every nook and corner of the world. Be it a political leader, a saint, a scholar, a preacher, whoever savours the nectar of his discourse, to him it has been a universal celebration. They have forgotten the bitter racism and immersed themselves in his 'Kadve Pravachan'.

After all, what is there in 'Kadve Pravachan?' Each word is a fierce spark, blistering amber and therefore they are 'Kadve Pravachan'. Fire burns but it gives light too; it also has the power to cook. Even if one spark enters your life, you too would be enlightened, charged and you would burn your sins and thus you would be able to see Him. Such collision gives birth to a flame. The wandering and lost mankind trapped between time and tradition, needs a medicine like 'Kadve Pravachan', to expel the toxins running through its veins and ruining the body. The first part of this book was published a few years back. It received accolades from all over the country and within a short span of a year and half, it sold off millions of prints which is a record. This is a world record in the history of Jainism. This is the entire part of 'Kadve Pravachan', which shows its progress. Every day, a new Sun representing new progressive steps rises on the horizon of your mind. May this Sun of 'Kadve Pravachan' help you to open your eyes! This is our auspicious wish and may you be blessed!

– Acharya Shri Pushpadant Sagar Ji

Digambar Muni- An Introduction

Munishree Tarunsagar Ji is a Digambar Jain Muni. Digambar means Dig+Ambar, which in Sanskrit means that the Directions themselves are his attire. It is not an easy task or childish act to be a Digambar Muni. It is a very difficult task and it is amazing too. Just by abandoning clothes, one cannot attain a Digambar Muni title. To become a Digambar Muni, every devotee has to fulfil 28 mammoth resolutions which are known as 28 basic virtues of a Muni belonging to Jainism.

A Jain Muni is like a god personified because of his austere behaviour. One cannot imagine how his entire life is full of sacrifice, penance, hard work, sacredness and dedication. You may not be aware that a Jain Digambar Muni partakes of food and water only once in 24 hours, and that too in a standing posture with both his palms made as a bowl- the 'Karapatra'. After this, he does not take even a drop of water irrespective of any circumstances.

Just remember that in extreme summer, when we feel thirsty after every ten minutes, he delivers discourses lasting for two hours at a stretch, walks over long distances and yet fulfils his vow. How difficult is this penance! Not only this, he does not go to any saloon for hair cutting but instead, after every four months, he plucks his hair from his head, beard and moustache. In Jain scriptures, this practice is called as 'Keshlonch'. Just try to pluck your hair, then only you will realize how hard a Digambar Jain Muni's penance is. In his whole life, he moves only on foot from place to place, he remains bare bodied in the harshest winter or summer. He bears a childlike detachment by winning over his body and mind. He does not bathe at all nor does he brush his teeth (He only gargles his mouth before his meal- only once a day!). He practises lifetime celibacy (Brahmacharya), keeps silence after sunset. He does not keep anything other than his peacock feather fan (picchi), kamandal (sacred bowl) and his scriptures.

The rules are very harsh for a Jain Muni. A common man cannot believe that he leads such a tough life. Dear Readers! A Digambar Muni not only goes around naked but when you observe his life, you will also conclude that no other person on this earth leads such tough life as that of a Digambar Muni.

You can understand how tough a Digambar Muni's life is by the very fact that among a million followers of Jain religion, there are only 500 Digambar Munis.

Revolutionary National Saint Jain Munishree Tarunsagar Ji had adopted the Jain Deeksha at a tender age of 13 and he has been following all the rules cited above since that time. Thus, he has been showing the right path of virtuousness to the entire world. That's really a commendable achievement and contribution to mankind!

....

I was reading a book. It was written in the book that you should offer food to the guest who visits your home. If you don't offer him food, offer him at least water. If you don't offer him water, you can offer at least a seat to him. If you don't offer him even a seat, you can at least talk to him in a sweet manner. Again, if you don't do this, you can have at least a smiling face. If you don't give him just a smile only, it is really a matter of utter shame on you; you must drown yourself in a palmful of water (to die from shame).

As dutiful parents, you must provide the best of education to your children and make them capable enough. Do not allow them to develop such an attitude that, in future, they may start thinking about you as 'worthless'. If you make this mistake today then you shall cry and regret when you get old tomorrow. I'm saying this because some people have committed this grave mistake in their life and are grieving today. There is no point crying over the Spilt milk?

The elderly should not interfere in the quarrel amongst children. Also, father and son should never intervene in the dispute between the mother-in-law and the daughter-in-law. It is very natural that the mother-in-law and the daughter-in-law would complain to their respective husbands in the night when they return home. Their husbands should lend patient ears to their complaints, also show sympathy but, they should adopt a policy of 'forget the past and move ahead' when they get up in the morning. Only then would the home remain united.

How it can be possible that life would be free from difficulties and obstacles. After all, there ought to be a Sunday every week. It is the law of Nature that you would get only that amount of joy and sorrow, which you are destined for and why would not it be? You shall reap only, what you sow. Remember that salt is also essential like sugar and it is natural that sorrow accompanies joy. Sorrow too is very important in our life. If there is no sorrow in your life, you would never remember God and would never seek His blessings.

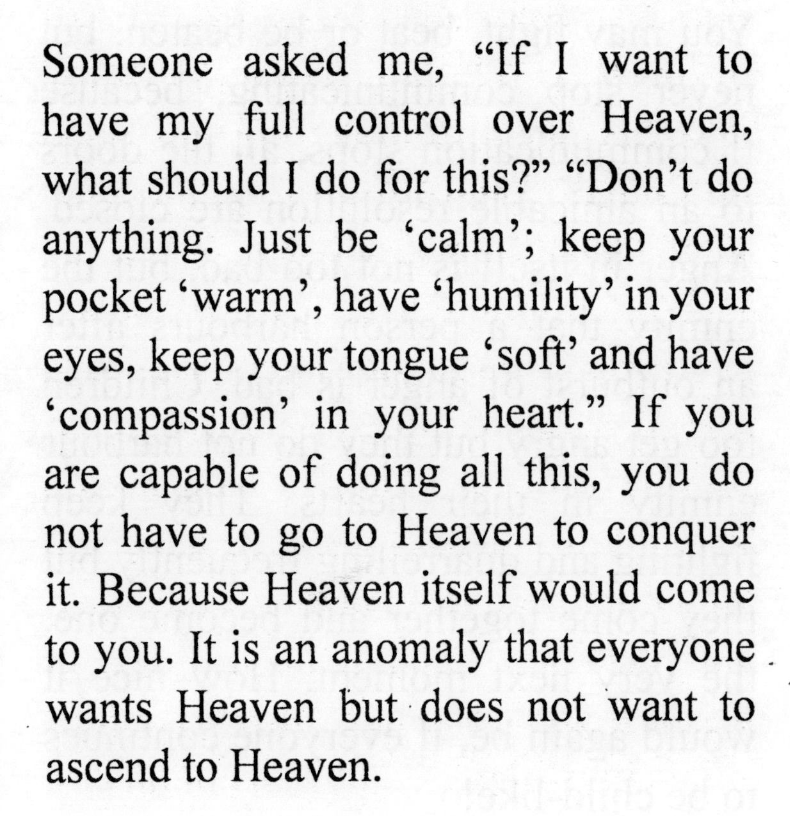

Someone asked me, "If I want to have my full control over Heaven, what should I do for this?" "Don't do anything. Just be 'calm'; keep your pocket 'warm', have 'humility' in your eyes, keep your tongue 'soft' and have 'compassion' in your heart." If you are capable of doing all this, you do not have to go to Heaven to conquer it. Because Heaven itself would come to you. It is an anomaly that everyone wants Heaven but does not want to ascend to Heaven.

You may fight, beat or be beaten, but never stop communicating, because if communication stops, all the doors to an amicable resolution are closed. Anger in itself is not too bad, but the enmity that a person harbours after an outburst of anger is bad. Children too get angry but they do not harbour enmity in their hearts. They keep fighting and quarrelling frequently but they come together and become one, the very next moment. How nice it would again be, if everyone continues to be child-like!

By living in this world, you must not forget two things. The first one– God, the Supreme Being and the second one– your death. At the same time, you ought to forget two things. The first one– if you have helped someone, and the second one– if somebody has done something wrong to you. Forget these things immediately. These are the only two things in this material world which are worth remembering and forgetting.

Death laughs loudly at two things. First, when the doctor tells the patient, "You need not worry; I am here to take care of you." And the second– When someone dies, and the other person says, "The poor fellow left for his heavenly abode." He says this in such a manner as if he would never die. Death laughs at his demeanour and says, "All right son! You called him 'Poor'. Don't worry; you'll also be having your turn any time. Is there anyone here who is not standing in the 'queue' of Death?"

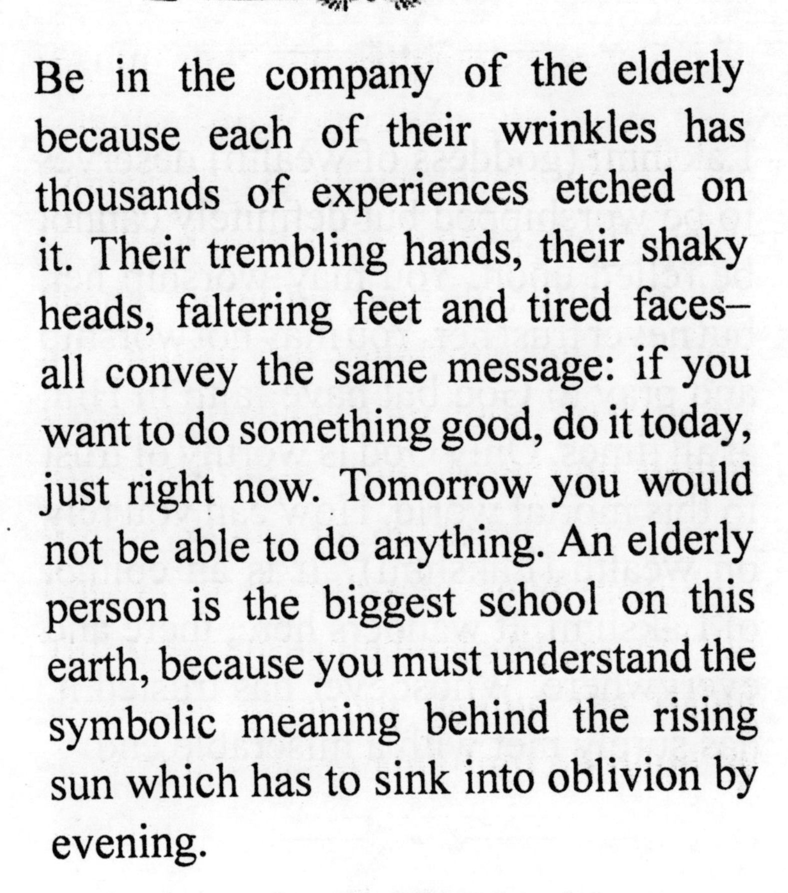

Be in the company of the elderly because each of their wrinkles has thousands of experiences etched on it. Their trembling hands, their shaky heads, faltering feet and tired faces– all convey the same message: if you want to do something good, do it today, just right now. Tomorrow you would not be able to do anything. An elderly person is the biggest school on this earth, because you must understand the symbolic meaning behind the rising sun which has to sink into oblivion by evening.

Lakshmi (goddess of wealth) deserves to be worshipped but definitely cannot be relied upon. You may worship her, but never trust her. You may not worship and pray to God but have faith in Him at all times. Only God is worthy of trust in this mortal world. How can you rely on wealth (Lakshmi)? It is an epithet of Lakshmi. It wanders here, there and everywhere. Whosoever has trusted it, has surely met with a miserable end.

Do not worry if any temple or mosque is destroyed; nor you should create a furore. Temples and mosques can be created and destroyed numerous times but if the temple of humanity is ruined even once, then nobody has the power to reconstruct it. Can bricks, mortar and cement made from soil be more expensive and precious than the bricks of humanity, mortar of character and cement of honesty?

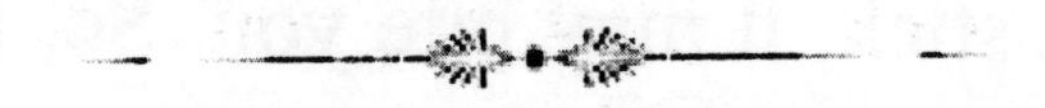

In today's time, dog-culture is speedily gaining momentum in our society. Earlier, people used to keep cows as pets; now they keep dogs. Once upon a time, our homes adored the sign on the outside wall– 'Atithi Devo Bhava'– The Guest is God. Then we followed it with 'Shubha-Labh'– An auspicious gain. As the time passed, we started writing 'Welcome'. And now it is written, 'Beware of dogs'. This is cultural degradation. Do feed a dog but do not love it. If you love it, it will lick your face and if you beat it with a stick, it may bite you. So, both its licking and biting are bad.

Learn to work hard and sweat it out. What you earn without hard work, sweat and pride, is illegitimate earnings. Do not live on interest which is illegitimate earnings because it does not require hard work, thus no sweating. But we are shrewd people. Although we gave up eating onions yet continue eating interest. To relish food bought from the income of interest is more sinful than eating onions. Earn your bread through sheer hard work and sweat. You can buy expensive bangles made of gold from illegitimate and sinful earnings, but it is also possible that for this you may have to wear iron handcuffs.

Anger has its own clan. It has a younger sister named Obstinacy. She always accompanies anger. Which has a wife named Violence. She always hides in the background but when she hears some commotion, she comes out. The name of Anger's elder brother is Ego. Anger also has a father and he is scared of him. His name is Fear. Ridicule and backbiting are Anger's daughters. One lives near his mouth while the other is near his ear. His son is named Enmity. Jealousy is the arrogant daughter-in-law of this family. This family has a grand-daughter named Hatred. She is always near the nose and frowning is her character. Contempt is the mother of anger.

I have never cremated a single corpse so far. Since I was very young, I had no occasion to go to the crematorium. In the initial days, I used to feel repentance for this. One day, I felt as if Lord Mahaveer had been saying to me, "Tarunsagar! You have been given this life, not to cremate the corpse but to instil life in seemingly dead people." From that day onwards, I have dedicated myself with all sincerity to instil life in human beings, society and nation, who are lying on the death-bed. Remember one thing– a half dead human being and a half dead society are worthless.

Form a habit of listening, because there is no dearth of people in this world who can speak a lot. Form a habit of living and smiling by swallowing bitter insults because the stock of nectar in this world has drastically reduced. Gather courage to face people who keep on blaming you because they will never be weary of calling your names. A critic is not bad; rather he acts like detergent-water in your life. Your life too needs a villain like we have in films. Your street seems to be cleaner if there are some pigs around.

There is nothing valuable than your mother, a saint and the Supreme Being– God, in your life. In your precious life, you need their blessings– of your mother's in the childhood, of a saint's in your youth and of God's in your old age. Your mother takes care of you in your childhood; if you go astray in your youth, the saint corrects you by giving you the right advice. The Mother, the Saint and God are everything in your life. If you delete these three words from religion, scriptures and history, then there would be nothing but a stock of worthless papers.

The path of truth is arduous. A thousand people think of treading on to this path but only a hundred can do it while nine hundred simply keep on thinking about it. Out of those hundred, who walked on this path only ten are able to reach, whereas the other ninety are lost on the way. Out of the ten who reach, only one attains the Ultimate Truth. The remaining nine are drawn at the border line. That is why it is said– there is one Ultimate Truth. Always remember that truth would never be defeated despite facing a lot of problems.

Today, it is a big challenge before the Jain community to continue the system of vegetarianism. During the last 2,500 years, after the salvation of Mahaveer, Jain community has been divided many times. This division was sometimes as Digambar Jain and Shwetamber Jain or Jainism with Terapanthi Jain or Beespanthi Jain. Now henceforth whenever there would be any division, it would not be such as Digambar Jain, Shwetamber Jain, Terapanthi Jain, Beespanthi Jain, Sthanakawasi Jain, Mandirmargi Jain; rather it would be such as 'Shakahari Jain' (Vegetarian Jain) and 'Mansahari Jain' (Non-vegetarian Jain). If this would ever to happen in reality, then remember Lord Mahaveer is not going to pardon us.

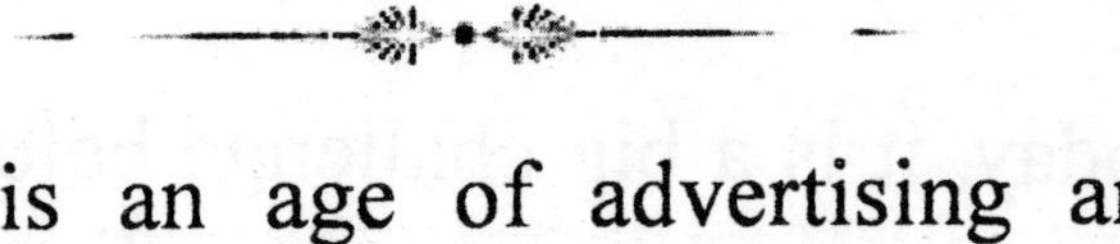

This is an age of advertising and marketing. Irrespective of the quality of merchandise being sold in any shop, if its packing and advertisement are not attractive, then that shop cannot do business. Jain religion is on backfoot due to this reason. Although the principles and values of Jain religion are great yet their presentation and marketing are not proper. Jain religion has the capacity to become 'Jana Dharma' (people's religion) due to its founding principles of Ahimsa (non-violence), Anekant (pluralism) and Aparigraha (non accumulation), but it has not progressed well and dumped, only due to lack of proper advertisement and publicity.

अहिंसा परमो धर्मः
यतो धर्मस्ततो जयः
सत्य
चरित्र
अपरिग्रह
अचौर्य
जिओ और जीने दो
भगवान महावीर स्वामी

संत मुरारी बापू

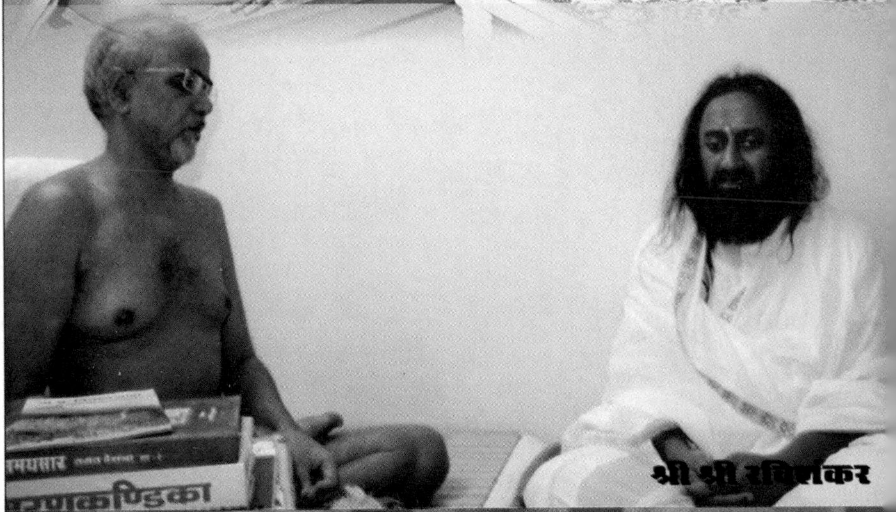

श्री श्री रविशंकर

योगगुरु रामदेव

सीआरपीएफ के जवानों को सम्बोधन
11 दिसं. 2009, रायपुर

मध्य प्रदेश विधानसभा
27 जुलाई 2010
क्रांतिकारी राष्ट्रसंत
का
मध्यप्रदेश
में

The Hindus and The Muslims are the two eyes of this great nation. For many centuries, they have been living together with love and affection, keeping hand in hand and marching ahead. Religious fanaticism does not run through the blood of this country and why is it so? When you write Ramzan, you start with 'Ram' and when you write Diwali you end with 'Ali'. Therefore, 'Ram' in Ramzan and 'Ali' in Diwali give us a message of living with love and peace. If all the devotees of Ram and Rahim use their wisdom then our country is no less than heaven on earth.

A crematorium should always be on the main square of the city; it should not be on the outskirts of the city. It should be located at the point where hundreds of people pass by every day and for ten times at least, so that whenever they pass through that point, the burning corpses and half burnt bodies may remind them of their own death. If this is being done, then seventy per cent of sin and crime would be vanished from this world. Today's a human being has forgotten that he too has to leave this world one day. Of course, you keep on saying that everyone has to die one day, but do you count yourself among them?

Export of 'animal-meat' is like butchering the economy of the nation. Export of meat puts a shameful blot on the forehead of our traditional culture of the ancient Rishis (sages) of India and its agricultural tradition. The government must stop this without any further delay and if it results into any losses to the economy of the nation, then we all religious leaders and saints would compensate this loss through our devotees. If the nation has to export something, then it should export 'compassion' and 'non-violence', milk and ghee, and virtues and traditions, etc. And if this is not possible then it would be better to export all the corrupt leaders so that the nation may be free from 'corruption'.

If you light a lamp before your deity, don't boast that you have lit the lamp. 'Oh! How can you ever light a lamp?' Two natural divine lamps always continue to glow before him at all times. The Sun shines during the day and the Moon in the night. How is your lamp going to compete with the Sun and the Moon? Then why is this ego? You have to think only as, "O God, I am worshipping the ocean with the water from a river and praying to the Sun through this little lamp. O God, I am surrendering to You all which is already yours."

No religion is bad but all religions have bad people who, for the sake of their selfish motives, hide behind religion and keep themselves engaged in their sinful activities and vile intentions. If we can change the hearts of these people, bring them on to the path of righteousness and teach them how to become honest human beings. Believe me, this earth would transform itself into heaven. Religion is not an ointment but it is a tonic. It should not be applied on the exterior; rather one has to drink it. It is really a big tragedy that we fight for religion, die for religion but do not try to become religious.

Religion is not such a headgear which you wear when you go to your shop and remove it once you reach there. Religion is like skin which you cannot separate from yourself. Religion is the very nature of its soul. Religion means love, compassion and fellow-feeling. Its symbol may be of Ram or Rahim, Buddha or Mahavir or Krishna or Karim, but everyone's soul will resound with the resonance of religion. Religion is not a wall; it's a door but when it becomes a wall then injustice and atrocities get a free playing field. Then, it does not matter if the wall belongs to a temple or a mosque.

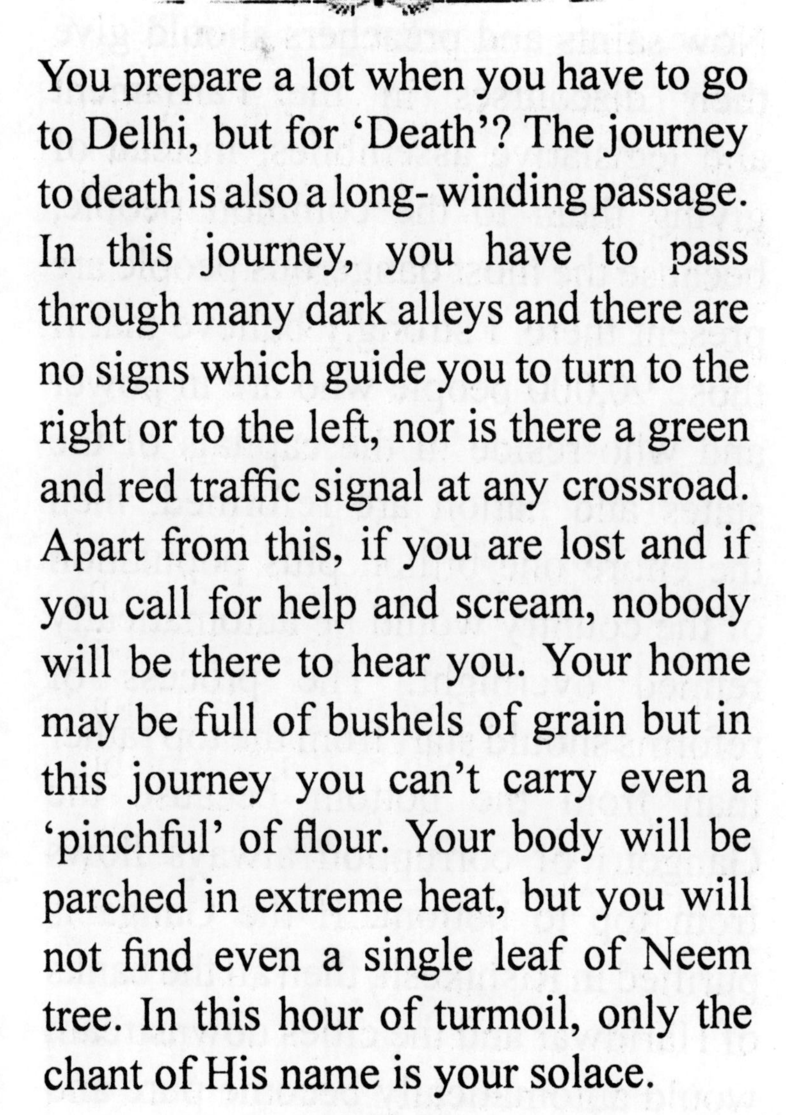

You prepare a lot when you have to go to Delhi, but for 'Death'? The journey to death is also a long- winding passage. In this journey, you have to pass through many dark alleys and there are no signs which guide you to turn to the right or to the left, nor is there a green and red traffic signal at any crossroad. Apart from this, if you are lost and if you call for help and scream, nobody will be there to hear you. Your home may be full of bushels of grain but in this journey you can't carry even a 'pinchful' of flour. Your body will be parched in extreme heat, but you will not find even a single leaf of Neem tree. In this hour of turmoil, only the chant of His name is your solace.

Now saints and preachers should give their discourses in the Parliament and legislative assemblies, instead of giving them to the common people, because the most dangerous people are present there. I strongly believe that if those 90,000 people who are in power and who reside in the capitals of the states and nation are reformed, then the entire one billion plus population of the country would be automatically refined overnight. The process of reforms should start from the top rather than from the bottom because the Gangotri of corruption always flows from top to bottom. If the Ganga is purified in Rishikesh, then all the banks of Haridwar and the cities downstream would automatically become pure and clean.

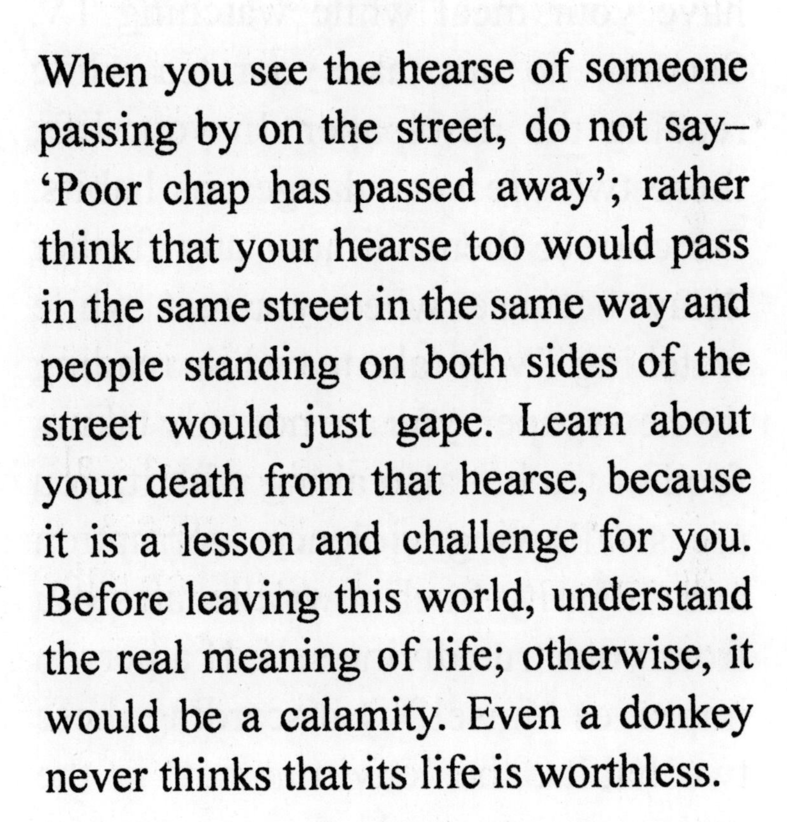

When you see the hearse of someone passing by on the street, do not say– 'Poor chap has passed away'; rather think that your hearse too would pass in the same street in the same way and people standing on both sides of the street would just gape. Learn about your death from that hearse, because it is a lesson and challenge for you. Before leaving this world, understand the real meaning of life; otherwise, it would be a calamity. Even a donkey never thinks that its life is worthless.

Be alert to two things. First, do not have your meal while watching TV. Second, do not take your tea while reading the newspaper. In your life, these two are very dangerous habits. Do correct them without any further delay because when you eat while watching TV or take tea while reading the newspaper, you are not only taking food or tea but also along with it, you are swallowing violence, corruption and vulgarity. Such news alienates you from your true divine self. If a person improves himself by discarding these two habits, the 'environment' in the entire society and country can be improved.

Food is very essential for survival. Water is more essential than food; air is more essential than water and life is more important than air, but nothing is required for death. A man can die by just sitting idle. A man does not always die due to the rupture of his brain's nerve or heart failure; even he dies on that day also when all his hopes and dreams get shattered; he loses his faith. In this way, a man dies even before his actual death and thus a man who is already dead does not die for the second time. How can it be possible?

If you are father, then the foremost responsibility you have towards your children is to make them so capable that they may deserve to be in the first row in the conference of saints and scholars. And if you are a son, then your foremost responsibility towards your father is to lead such a pure and ideal life that the whole world is going to ask your father which penance and philanthropic deeds he did which gave him such a capable and virtuous son like you.

If you want to transform your home into heaven, then the husband and wife, the mother-in-law and the daughter-in-law, and the father and the son will have to come to an agreement that if one of them becomes fire, the other would play the role of water. Always have some water in your home because you never know when your heart would start emitting the fire of anger. Anger is fire. Always keep ready with the water of tolerance and peace in your home. You do not know when your home would be engulfed in the flames of anger. Always keep in mind– whenever a husband becomes the fire of anger, then his wife should become 'water' to extinguish it. Similarly, when a wife becomes the fire of anger, then her husband should become 'water current'.

It is said that a child is more influenced by his mother, but these days, the child is more influenced by media as compared to his mother. In the past, it was said that the child was following into the footsteps of either his mother or father. But these days, the manner in which the local and foreign channels are serving the face of violence and vulgarity, then that day is not very far when we will start saying that one child has followed into the footsteps of Zee TV, while the other child craves for Star TV, and still the third one is a die-hard fan of Fashion TV. Now-a-days the cultural assaults made by various channels on our nation are more dangerous than the terrorist attacks of Osama Bin Laden.

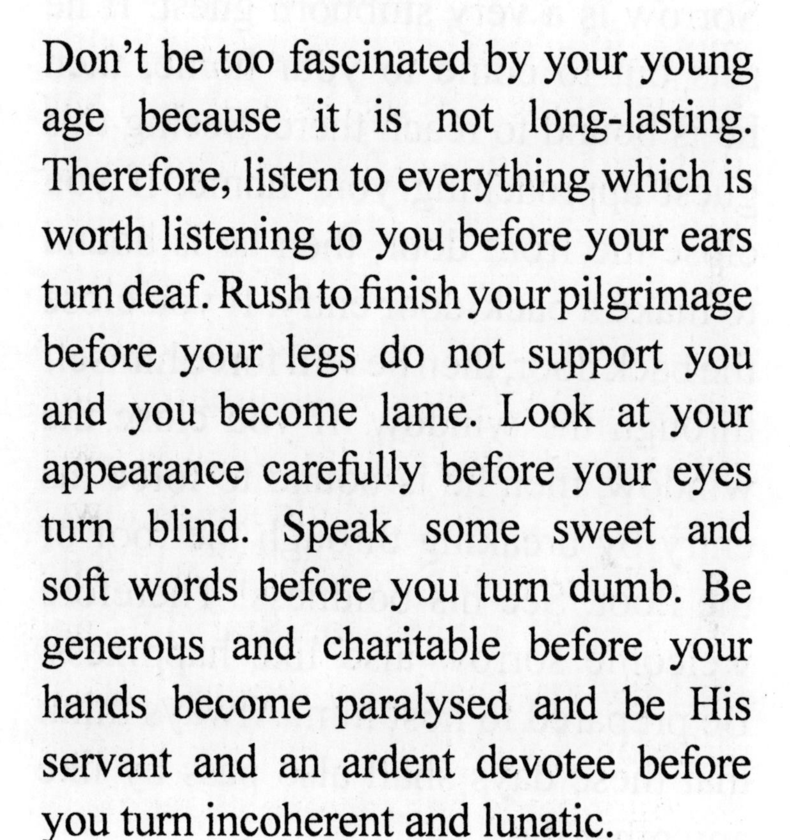

Don't be too fascinated by your young age because it is not long-lasting. Therefore, listen to everything which is worth listening to you before your ears turn deaf. Rush to finish your pilgrimage before your legs do not support you and you become lame. Look at your appearance carefully before your eyes turn blind. Speak some sweet and soft words before you turn dumb. Be generous and charitable before your hands become paralysed and be His servant and an ardent devotee before you turn incoherent and lunatic.

Sorrow is a very stubborn guest. If he sets out to come to your home, then he is bound to reach there. Seeing this guest approaching your home, if you close the front door, then he is bound to make a back-door entry. If you close the back door, then he will force himself through the window. If you close the window, then he is bound to force his entry by breaking through the roof or the floor. See his boldness! Therefore welcome sorrow also like happiness. Be prepared to host him. Always think that these days shall also pass by like any other day.

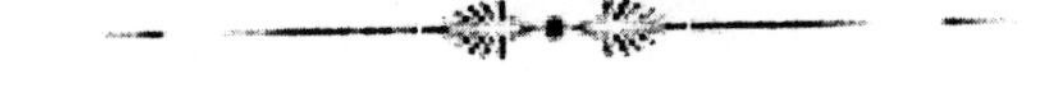

If an engineer is corrupt, then few bridges or buildings would prematurely collapse. If a doctor is corrupt, then some people may die untimely. But if a teacher is corrupt, then the entire future generation would get ruined. Today the future of the nation is in the hands of teachers, because the new generation is sitting on their doorsteps to learn something. If the entire population of one crore and eighty lakh teachers of this nation decide to contribute then by 2020 India is going to be transformed into not only a 'Developed Nation' but also a 'Global Nation'.

There is nothing unusual if your son takes care of you. Of course, he has to do, because after all your blood runs through his veins. But if your daughter-in-law takes care of you, then it is surprising. Leave alone her being your blood relative, she is not even distantly related to you. Despite this if she serves you then it is bound to be the fruit of your good deeds in some previous births. In this era, people are lucky to relish many kinds of comforts but there are very few parents who have the rare and good fortune to relish the joy of being served by their sons and daughters-in-law.

Follow the religion of serving your neighbourhood. What is this religion? It means that while you eat, you should also remember that your neighbour should never starve. A good neighbour is like a blessing. You should never spoil your relations with him, because we may live without our friends but not without our neighbours. Be his companion in his joy and grief. The reason is– if his home catches fire, then you must understand that your property is also in danger. And yes, if you give him something as a matter of small courtesy, you can be confident to get it back in ample measure.

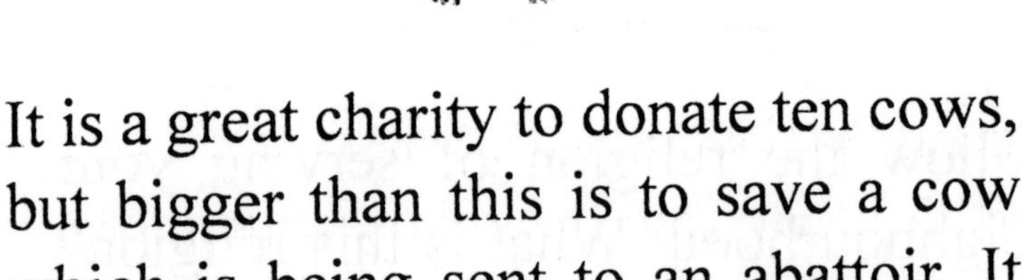

It is a great charity to donate ten cows, but bigger than this is to save a cow which is being sent to an abattoir. It is an act of charity to construct ten temples but a bigger charity than this is to renovate an ancient one. To renovate ten ancient temples is really a big charity but bigger than this is to transform a terrorist to follow the path of non-violence. If you turn a non-vegetarian person into a vegetarian one, with you inspiration, then you can be proud of attaining the reward of virtue by completing the pilgrimage of all the four holy places without leaving your home.

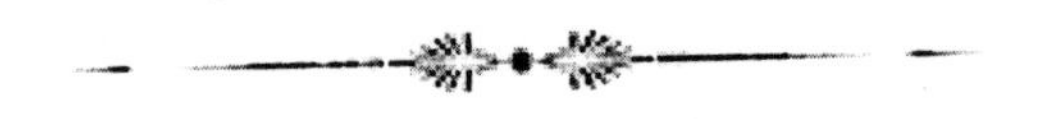

Recently I went to Surat. There, one old woman said to me, "Munishree, your arrival has caused me a lot of difficulties." I asked her, "Why is it so?" The old woman said, "My daughter-in-law and I used to go daily to listen to a 'discourse' in the morning, 'religious debate' in the afternoon and to watch a 'holy procession' in the evening." I said, "Isn't that a good thing? Then why are you being so panic?" The old woman said, "Ever since you have come to Surat, I hardly find any time to fight with my daughter-in-law." I said, "Amma! It means Muni Tarunsagar's visit to Surat and your visit to 'holy discourse' have become worthwhile."

There are four kinds of sons. The first one is the lender son. He was your lender in the previous birth and now he is born to you as your son. Now, in this birth, you have to pay for his education, get him married and clear his debt and then he will die. The second one is the enemy son. In the last birth, he was your enemy and now born to you as your son. At every turn in your life, he gives you pain and sorrow. The third one is an indifferent son. He gives you neither joy nor sorrow. Such a son is a name-sake only. The fourth one is a servant son. In the previous birth, you were good to someone and served him. Now in this life, he is born as your son. Such a son gives a lot of joy and happiness to his parents.

A beggar, who was lame, was always happy and cheerful. Someone asked him, “O brother, you are not only a beggar but also lame; you don’t have any possessions as well; still, you are so happy. How can it be?” He replied, “Babuji! I am grateful to Him that, at least, I am not blind. Yes, I cannot walk, but I can see this world. I do not complain to Him for something which I did not get, but I always thank Him for what He has blessed me with.” This is an art of discovering joy out of sorrow.

You must hand over your earnings what you have earned through your hard work, sweat and toil to your better half because she is the true Lakshmi (goddess of wealth) residing in your home. That Lakshmi, which is in your safe box, is standing all alone in one place but this Lakshmi residing with you in your home is your partner throughout your life. A person who takes alcohol by spending money (Dhanalakshmi) in the market, comes home and insults his Grihalakshmi, uses abusive language and physically assaults her, will be deprived of both the Lakshmis in his life. The goddess Lakshmi from the safe walks out from the front door, and the Grihalakshmi walks out from the back door.

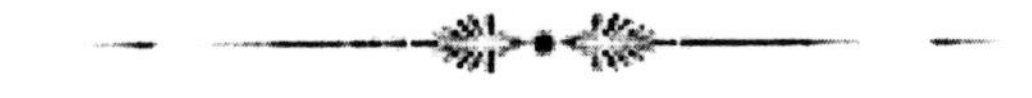

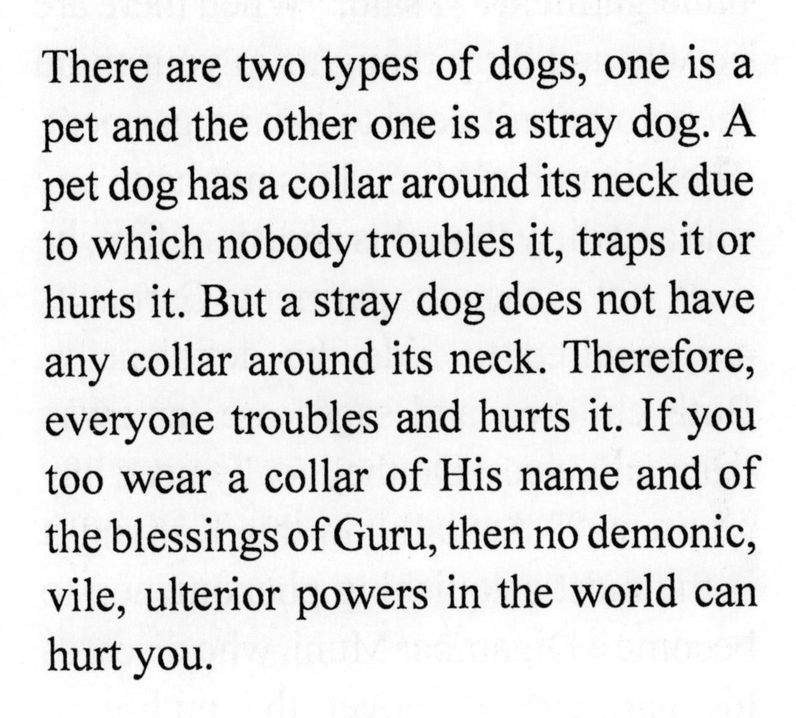

There are two types of dogs, one is a pet and the other one is a stray dog. A pet dog has a collar around its neck due to which nobody troubles it, traps it or hurts it. But a stray dog does not have any collar around its neck. Therefore, everyone troubles and hurts it. If you too wear a collar of His name and of the blessings of Guru, then no demonic, vile, ulterior powers in the world can hurt you.

Someone asked me, “Why does a Digambar Muni not wear any undergarment?” I said, “When there are no vile and dirty thoughts in your mind then you don’t need to wear a garment. The Digambar Muni does not have any vile and dirty thoughts and, therefore, he does not wear any garment. Garments are required to hide the deficiencies. Both children and sages are far away from any vices. Do they really need any garments?” Actually, in this Kaliyug it is the most astonishing phenomenon to become a Digambar Muni, who discards his garments to cover the nudity of the society. He is that ‘Digamber Jain Muni’.

Every morning, you must start your day with a small prayer. You must ask him, 'O Lord, bless me so as to become the feet of the lame and eyes to the blind. May my arms be the support for the helpless and may my tongue always console my brethren who are in grief and turmoil! Bless me with power to shed my sweat in the service of the poor and the sick. Let no guest return hungry from my door-step. My Lord! Make this child of Yours to be like this at all times. O Supreme Being! Please accept my humble obeisance.'

Pups and foals also have parents at the time of their birth. However, very few children are fortunate to have such cultured parents who bring them up properly. Lucky are those children whose parents have not only taught them how to walk by holding their fingers but also taught them how to pray at a temple. Do not just carry your children on the shoulders and cuddle them in your lap; instead, admit them in the school of cultures. Even a bitch takes care of its pup's comfort and happiness. A mother, in real sense, is the one who gets worried not only about her child's comfort but also about his/her good cultural values.

There are so many evils in the world, but why? Because good people are not carrying out their responsibilities. Good people have started living for themselves in their own cocoon of solitude. In order to protect their reputation and prestige, they are giving up their responsibilities and making their seats vacant, thus facilitating the entry of evil people. Do remember– No chair of position will ever fall vacant. If good people are not going to occupy it, then it is natural that the evil shall grab it and it shall have the reins of command. This is only happening in our country today. You can see the consequences!

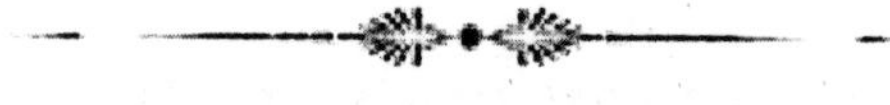

I think that instead of matching the horoscope of the bride and the bridegroom, before the marriage, one must match the horoscope of the bride and her would-be mother-in-law. The reason is very apparent. Only they have to face each other throughout the day. What is the need to match the horoscope of the bride and the bridegroom then that would otherwise match? For a happy marriage, the bride and the bridegroom should take only one vow at the time of their marriage, that is, "If I become fire, you play the role of water and if you become an ember, I will be the spring of water."

It is natural to have food when you are hungry, and to eat without hunger is abnormality and a disease. To remain hungry while feeding the other hungry person is a culture. When you eat, do not think that you are eating; rather consider it as you are making an offering to Him Who dwells within you. If you start thinking in this way then you will not consume meat, tobacco, alcohol. Do you ever offer these as 'Prasad' to God? A big 'No'! Then why do you insult Him by putting them into your stomach? Do remember that He resides within you.

If you are a mother-in-law and you want peace and happiness in your family, then pay attention to four points. First, do not differentiate between your daughter and daughter-in-law. Treat your daughter-in-law like your daughter. Second, if you ever have a quarrel with your daughter-in-law, then don't blame her parents. She will never tolerate it. Third, do not blame her by sitting at a temple; otherwise, you will close all the doors to an amicable solution. Fourth, always pay attention to what your daughter-in-law wants, because after all "A mother-in-law was also a daughter-in-law".

भारतीय-सेना (मराठा इन्फेन्ट्री) को सम्बोधन 21 सितं. 2005, बेलगांव (कर्ना.)

सेना द्वारा 'गार्ड-ऑफ-आर्नर' का सम्मान

28 अप्रैल 2013, भीलवाड़ा (राज.)

The secret of happy life is to feel happy and enjoy with whatever you have; do not get mad for those things which you do not have. For example, if you have ₹ 90 in your pocket, feel happy about it. Do not feel sad for the balance of ten rupees which would make it a hundred rupees. Do not get carried away by speculating that it would become hundred. Probably you will never be able to fulfil desire to get a hundred rupees and it is also likely that you may lose the ninety rupees which you already have. Emperor Alexander the Great also could not reach hundred years of life. Then where are you standing? You are nothing when compared to him. You are the 'commonest of the common'.

We are having many living rooms and a toilet in our house; a person should give the same amount of time in politics which he spends in the toilet. Actually, in your day-to-day life, the importance of politics should never be more than a 'toilet' at any cost. If you keep water in the refrigerator for too long, it turns into ice and a man who is entrenched in politics, day and night, also becomes corrupt.

If you are a student, then take care of my advice very carefully. Do not waste any time when you are in the tenth and the twelth standard, put in your best efforts because these are the two years which mould your career. If you sleep for these two years then you have to remain awake throughout your whole life. You will be forced to lead your life by doing treacherous and laborious work and if you stay alert in these classes, burn the midnight oil, work hard and acquire success in your studies then you can lead a comfortable life. You will get a good job and good position, so you will be leading your life very comfortably.

Once I saw that a lizard was hanging upside down from the roof of my room. I asked, "What is the matter? Why are you hanging upside down?" The lizard said, "Munishree! I am holding and supporting this roof. If I move away, the roof shall crumble." This lizard is none other than 'YOU' only. You are also living with this delusion that only you are carrying the responsibility of your family on your shoulders; otherwise, everything would collapse. Do remember– if anybody moves from this world, the life will still move on.

Do you want to get angry or you want to seek revenge? Then do not be in a hurry to do it. Instead, go to an astrologer and tell him that you want to get angry and also want to take his revenge on his enemy, so find out an auspicious day for it. When you look for an auspicious day for an auspicious deed, then why don't you look for an auspicious day to carry out an inauspicious deed? That way 'Amrityog' in the 'Pushya Nakshatra' is the most auspicious day to spurt your anger, but the only problem is that it comes only twice in a year. Now what's your viewpoint?

When you were too young and you were not earning any money, then your father used to provide you with 'pocket money' for your personal expenses. Now when you are grown up, have started earning and your father has grown old, so you should give 'pocket money' to him. A part of whatever you earn should be given with humility and you must say, "My revered father! Everything which I am earning is all yours, so please accept this as a 'token' of it and bless me."

If your son hangs your beautiful portrait on the wall of the drawing room, then do not feel too happy about it. Instead, think that now the portrait is hung on the wall, God knows when this would be accompanied with a garland. So, before a garland is going to be put on the portrait, surrender yourself at the feet of the Lord and start chanting His name. His rosary is your wealth, and no other wealth is worth for you. It is not enough that He is good and true, but you must feel His belongingness with you.

One must have an art to discover 'lyrics' from 'abuses'. If you learn and become master in this art, then no abuse can make you angry. For example, there was a fight between the husband and the wife. The wife called her husband 'Jaanvar' (animal). Later she asked, "I called you 'Jaanvar'; did you not feel bad?" The husband said, "No." The wife asked again, "Why?" The husband replied, "Aren't you my 'Jaan' (life)?" The wife said, "Yes." The husband added, "Am I not your 'Var' (husband) ?" The wife said, "Yes." "So, in this way, aren't we both 'Jaanvars'."

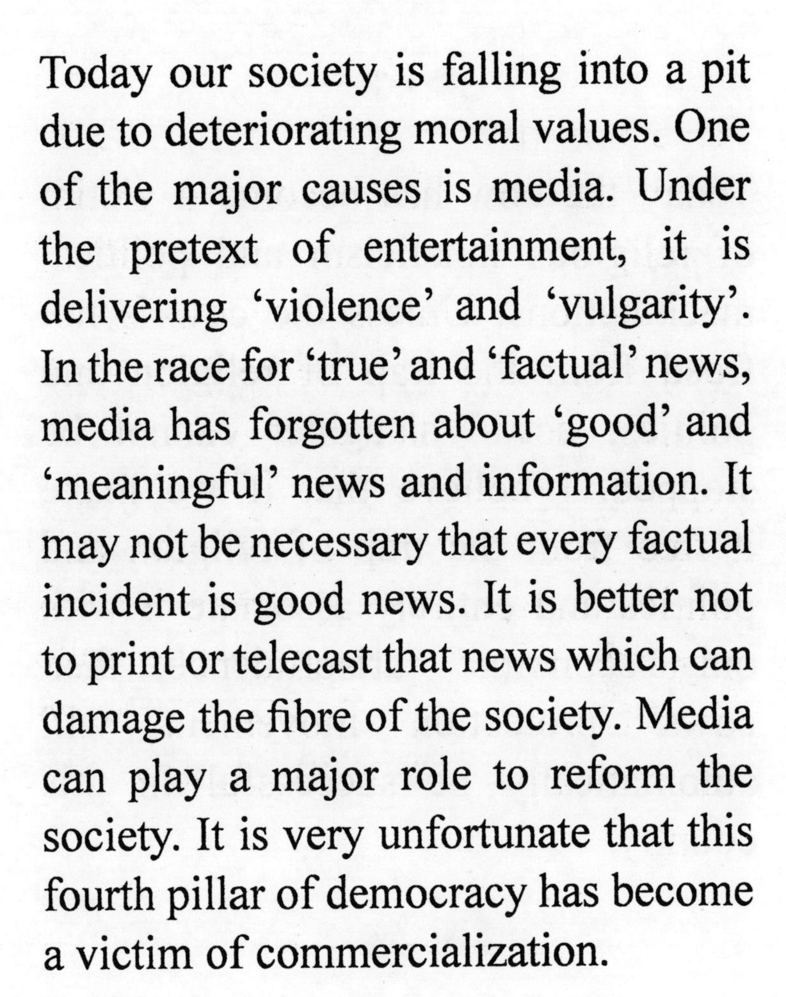

Today our society is falling into a pit due to deteriorating moral values. One of the major causes is media. Under the pretext of entertainment, it is delivering 'violence' and 'vulgarity'. In the race for 'true' and 'factual' news, media has forgotten about 'good' and 'meaningful' news and information. It may not be necessary that every factual incident is good news. It is better not to print or telecast that news which can damage the fibre of the society. Media can play a major role to reform the society. It is very unfortunate that this fourth pillar of democracy has become a victim of commercialization.

Today the cow has become a victim of religious fanaticism and political machinations. Unless the cow is not freed from the trap of religion and politics, cows' slaughter cannot be stopped. I believe that if we make it free from the trap of religion and politics and entirely associate it with only economic jurisprudence, then cows' protection movement will automatically be successful in this country.

If you are parents and thinking of getting your son married, I may suggest you to bring a daughter-in-law instead of 'Bahurani', *i.e.* the queen daughter-in-law. When only a daughter-in-law comes home, she would bring 'good culture' *(Sanskar)* along with her and if you bring Bahurani, she would bring a 'car' with her, and it is dead sure that she would like to rule there. And the one who brings 'good culture' would be at your beck and call. Moreover, she would groom your son in such a way that your life would be like heaven and a 'Bahurani' would influence your son in such a way that you live like a 'dead' person even while you are alive.

Both the saint and the policeman work towards the reformation of society; only difference is that the saint makes you understand by the language of 'symbolism' while the policeman makes you understand by the language of 'baton'. In fact, those who do not understand the language of 'symbols' given by saints, need to be treated with the baton of a policeman. The uniform of a policeman is no less important than the saffron clothes of a saint. A uniform is a symbolic representation of 'faith'. If a uniformed person supports corruption then he fragments the pride of a uniform.

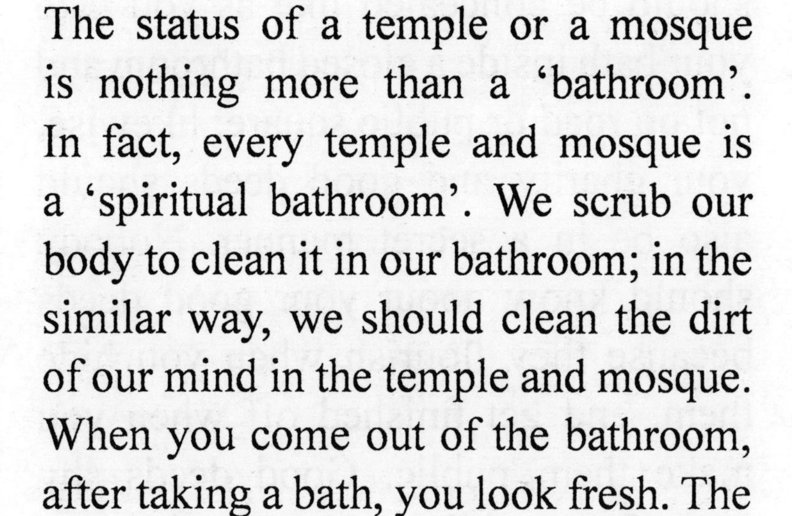

The status of a temple or a mosque is nothing more than a 'bathroom'. In fact, every temple and mosque is a 'spiritual bathroom'. We scrub our body to clean it in our bathroom; in the similar way, we should clean the dirt of our mind in the temple and mosque. When you come out of the bathroom, after taking a bath, you look fresh. The same freshness, humility and peace should reflect on your face when you come out of any temple or mosque.

Charity and good deeds should be carried out in solitude. Your charity should be concealed like as you take your bath inside a closed bathroom and not on road or public square; likewise, your charity and good deeds should also be in a secret manner. Nobody should know about your good deeds because they flourish when you hide them, and get finished off when you make them public. Good deeds shy away from publicity. You should carry out your charity and good deeds by 'hiding' them and not by 'publicizing' them. If there is garbage inside your house and you want to throw it, then do you advertise it in the newspaper?

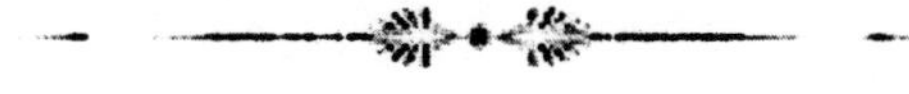

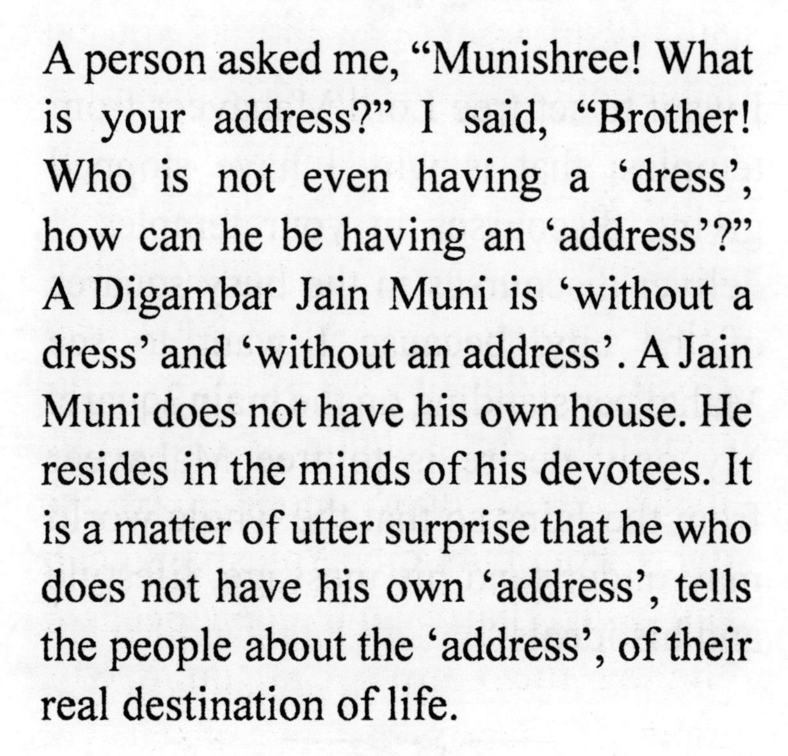

A person asked me, "Munishree! What is your address?" I said, "Brother! Who is not even having a 'dress', how can he be having an 'address'?" A Digambar Jain Muni is 'without a dress' and 'without an address'. A Jain Muni does not have his own house. He resides in the minds of his devotees. It is a matter of utter surprise that he who does not have his own 'address', tells the people about the 'address', of their real destination of life.

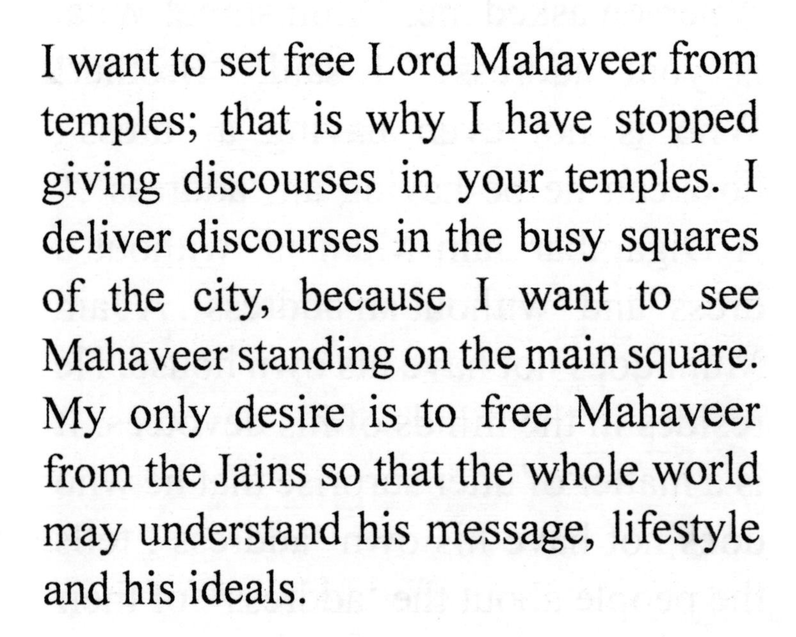

I want to set free Lord Mahaveer from temples; that is why I have stopped giving discourses in your temples. I deliver discourses in the busy squares of the city, because I want to see Mahaveer standing on the main square. My only desire is to free Mahaveer from the Jains so that the whole world may understand his message, lifestyle and his ideals.

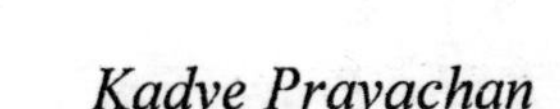

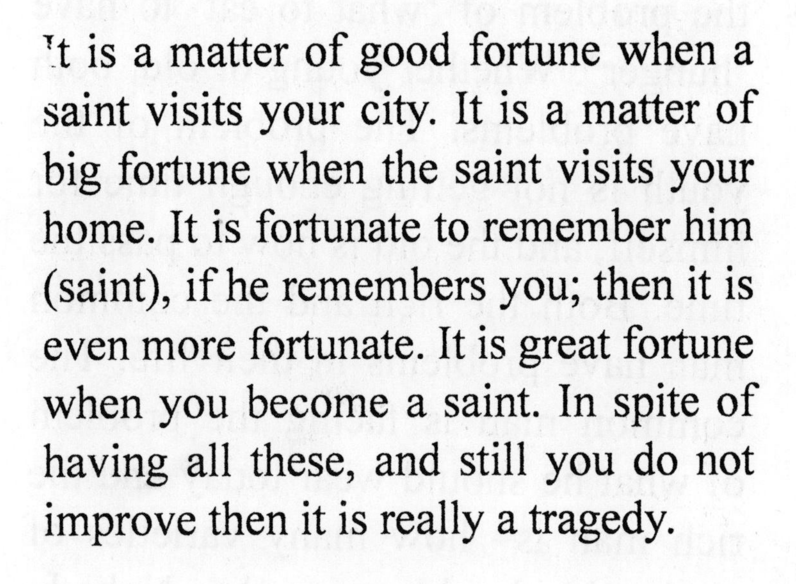

It is a matter of good fortune when a saint visits your city. It is a matter of big fortune when the saint visits your home. It is fortunate to remember him (saint), if he remembers you; then it is even more fortunate. It is great fortune when you become a saint. In spite of having all these, and still you do not improve then it is really a tragedy.

Both the rich and the poor have the same problem. A poor man is having the problem of 'what to eat' at the time of 'hunger', and a rich man is having the problem of 'what to eat' to have 'hunger'. Whether young or old, both have problems. The problem of the youth is not getting enough time for himself, and the old is how to pass the time. Both the rich and the common man have problems in their life. The common man is facing the problem of what he should wear today and the rich man is– how many varieties of clothes he should wear today. Nobody is content in this world. The Poor want to be rich and the rich want to be beautiful. Bachelors want to marry, while the married persons want to die.

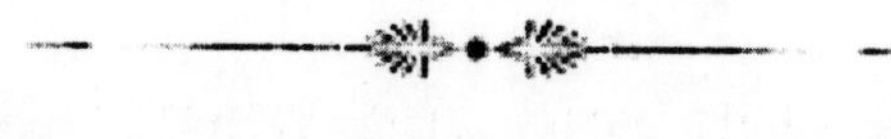

To smile is an act of benevolence and to make someone laugh is a bigger benevolence. When you smile, it is like a prayer to God, but when you bring smile to someone who is crying then God prays for you. When you cry, tears are there, but you don't need tears when you smile. Then why don't you smile? We must smile, but it should not be a malicious and sarcastic smile like 'Mama Shakuni'; it should rather be an innocent and pure one like a child or a saint. Actually, in true sense, only two kinds of people laugh. One is a lunatic, while the other one is a supremely pure soul. The remaining people either cry or pretend to laugh.

One question is often asked of me, "What is the secret of a happy life?" The secret of a happy life is to spend your day in such a way that you could sleep well in the night, and spend each night in such a way that you should not be ashamed to show your face in the morning. To live your young days in such a way, that you do not have to repent in your old age, and plan your old age in such a way, that you do not have to beg before others.

If you use your vehicle, then you have to send it to a garage for its service as well. Why? In order to clean and keep it in a good condition. The religious meetings of the saints are like a garage, where your mind and brain are cleansed like an engine. Life too is a vehicle– a vehicle of determination. If this vehicle has the wheels of courage, an engine of religiosity, fuel of hard work, steering wheel of restraint, accelerator of decorum, brakes of discipline and the tool box carries the instruments of philosophy, knowledge and character, then this vehicle definitely reaches the destination of salvation, sooner or later.

I have heard this recently: One evening, there was a fight between a husband and a wife. At night, the husband gave a slip of paper to his wife, on which it was written– I have to go to Mumbai tomorrow. The train is at 6 am, so wake me up at 5 am." The husband slept comfortably, after giving that slip. When he got up in the morning, it was 8 o' clock. He got highly infuriated. Just then, he saw a slip lying near by. It read, "Dear husband, it is 5 am now; please wake up." Now; this is the real situation of husband-wife; they still claim– "Kaho Na...Pyaar hai." The situation of Indo-Pak, still, states– "Hum Saath-Saath Hain." So, this is not an ideal conjugal relationship.

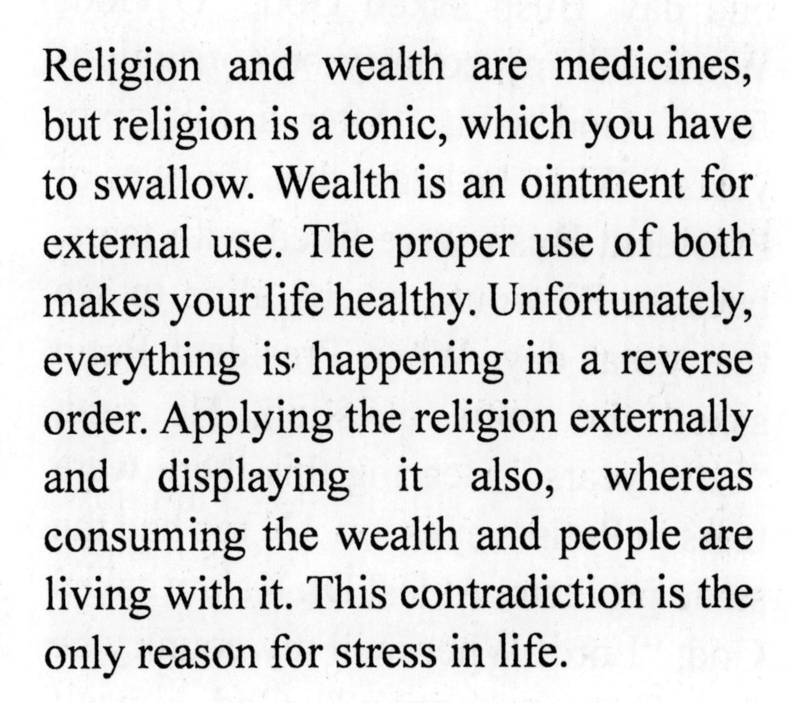

Religion and wealth are medicines, but religion is a tonic, which you have to swallow. Wealth is an ointment for external use. The proper use of both makes your life healthy. Unfortunately, everything is happening in a reverse order. Applying the religion externally and displaying it also, whereas consuming the wealth and people are living with it. This contradiction is the only reason for stress in life.

I have heard this: The Presidents of America, Russia and India met God one day. Bush asked God, "O God! When will my country be corruption-free?" God said, "After a full sixty years." When he heard this, the eyes of President Bush were filled with tears, because he would not be alive to see that great day. When President Putin asked the same question, He said, "Fifty years." Hearing this there were tears in Putin's eyes too. He too had the same problem. At last Dr. Kalam asked God, "Lord! When will my country be free from corruption?" God himself had tears in His eyes when He heard the question. Isn't this very serious?

Jain religion is very 'strong', but it never displays its strength. To understand it, you need a kind heart, not mind. Non-violence, pluralism and non-possessiveness, in your day-to-day life, are the essence of Jain religion. If you want to describe the essence of Jainism in one word, it is 'Veetaragata-non-attachment'. Jain religion does not encourage the worship of an individual but inspires you to worship personality. This religion does not only transform its followers into devotees but also permits them to become deities themselves. Jain religion is like a glittering diamond, but unfortunately it has fallen into the hands of unscrupulous coal merchants.

You should harbour a feeling of benevolence in your mind for someone who hurts you and also thinks ill of you. Try to forgive him. The reason is that he was your brother in some previous life. If your teeth cut your tongue, then do you break your teeth? Not at all. Then why do you get furious over the mistake of your own brother? You also do not know there is a villain behind every great soul. Do not be afraid of critics. After all, stones are pelted only to those trees, which bear sweet fruits.

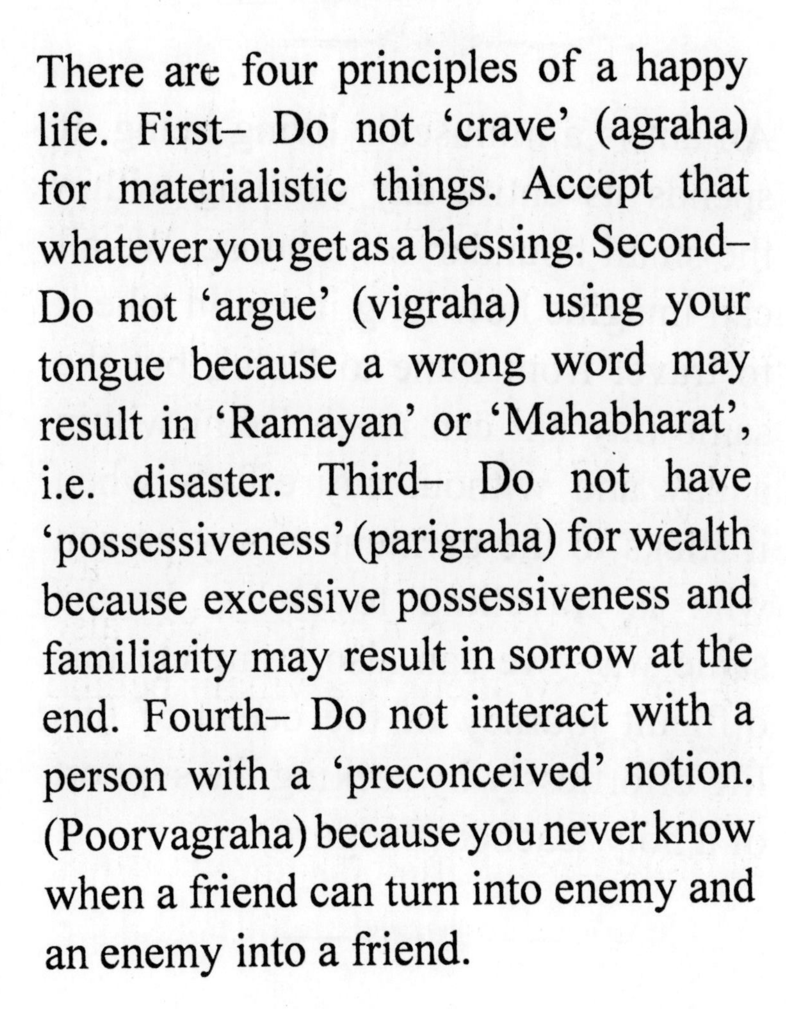

There are four principles of a happy life. First– Do not 'crave' (agraha) for materialistic things. Accept that whatever you get as a blessing. Second– Do not 'argue' (vigraha) using your tongue because a wrong word may result in 'Ramayan' or 'Mahabharat', i.e. disaster. Third– Do not have 'possessiveness' (parigraha) for wealth because excessive possessiveness and familiarity may result in sorrow at the end. Fourth– Do not interact with a person with a 'preconceived' notion. (Poorvagraha) because you never know when a friend can turn into enemy and an enemy into a friend.

An ant is a minuscule living being. It spends its entire day strolling within the small boundary of a house. We all can imagine how long it would take it to travel from Pune to Delhi, but the same tiny ant can reach Delhi within a day and without any efforts when it sticks to the garment of any person who is travelling to Delhi. In the same way, we can also complete this difficult journey of the ocean of this life effortlessly by seeking the support of a holy teacher (Sadguru).

I pray to Him every day for one thing and I insist on you also offering similer prayer before Him. I pray to Him in respect that every day at least one human being should be born in this world who has strong determination like Mahaveer– Buddha, glory like Rama–Krishna, devotion like Kundakunda–Kabir and simplicity like Gandhi and Vivekananda. And more so, every day at least one human being should leave this world like Mahaveer, whose death becomes a matter of celebration like 'Diwali', and more so becomes 'Mahaveer's salvation(nirvana)' celebration. If you want to learn to live, learn it from the Geeta and if you want to learn to die, then learn it from Mahaveer.

A passenger who has more luggage finds too many difficulties during travelling in a train. He faces more problems in boarding as well as alighting from the train. This reality very much applies to the journey of life as well. If we travel in the journey of life with excess of wealth, then we will face enormous difficulties, when we reach the destination of death. To make the journey of life happy, stay away from excessive accumulation (Ati-parigraha) and excessive acquaintances (Ati-parichaya).

There are three deities in this world– Brahma, Vishnu and Mahesh. Brahma is the originator, therefore people worship him. Vishnu is the protector and Mahesh is the destroyer provider, therefore people prostrate before them. Brahma, Vishnu and Mahesh cannot be merged with one another, but in this world there is an element called mother which has all the three, namely Brahma, Vishnu and Mahesh. A mother gives birth, therefore she is Brahma, she nurtures and brings up her children, therefore she is Vishnu and she gives them good teaching and virtues, therefore she is Mahesh as well. Tie a boulder weighting five kg on your stomach just for nine hours and you will come to know what a mother is.

Once a saint knocked at the door and demanded, "Bhiksham dehi." A small girl came out and said, "Baba! We are poor; we have nothing to give." The saint said, "My child! Please do not turn me away; you can give me the soil from your front courtyard." The girl picked up a fistful of soil and put it in his bowl. The disciple asked, "Guruji! It is not the alms. Why did you ask her to do so?" The saint said, "My son! If she had refused today, she would not have been able to give in future. What happened if she has given today? At least she has learnt the art of giving. Today she has given the soil, tomorrow she would give fruits and flowers as well. Always lead a life of a donor."

जैन-मुनि या जन-मुनि ?

गाँधी ही गाँधी
ऐसा नज़ारा आपने
पहले कभी देखा ?

गिनीज बुक ऑफ वर्ल्ड
रिकॉर्ड में दर्ज हुई
'अहिंसा दांडी यात्रा'

इतिहास में पहली बार किसी दिगम्बर जैन मुनि का नाम 'गिनीज़ वर्ल्ड रिकॉर्ड' में और उनके द्वारा लिखी गई 'कड़वे-प्रवचन' पुस्तक का नाम 'लिम्का बुक ऑफ रिकॉर्ड' में दर्ज हुआ।

आहारदान

मुख्यमंत्री श्री शिवराज सिंह चौहान सपत्नीक द्वारा आहार दान, मुख्यमंत्री निवास, भोपाल (म.प्र.)

मुख्यमंत्री डॉ. रमनसिंह सपत्नीक द्वारा आहार दान, मुख्यमंत्री निवास, रायपुर (छ.ग.)

श्री ईश्वरदास रोहाणी (म.प्र. विधानसभा अध्यक्ष) द्वारा आहार दान (जबलपुर, म.प्र.)

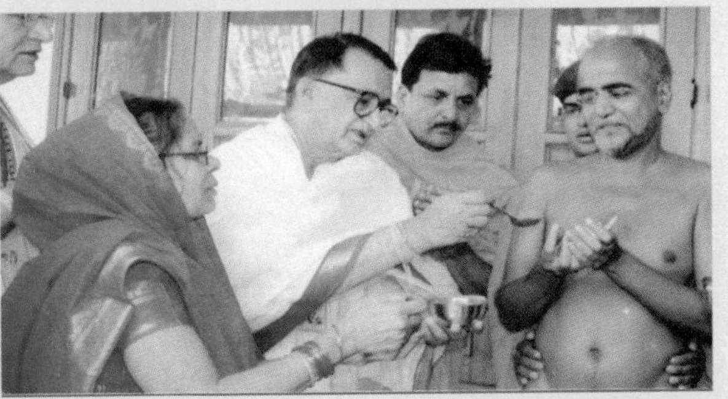

ठा. हरवंशसिंह, म.प्र. विधानसभा उपाध्यक्ष द्वारा आहार दान बर्रा (सिवनी, म.प्र.)

मुनिश्री तरुणसागरजी दिगम्बर मुनि हैं। दिगम्बर मुनि का जीवन अत्यन्त तपश्यापूर्ण होता है। वे 24 घंटे में सिर्फ एक बार अन्न-जल ग्रहण करते हैं वह भी खड़े-खड़े अपनी दोनों अजुंली को 'कर-पात्र' बनाकर।

Before going to sleep at night, 'Review' your day's events. Appreciate your achievements (whatever you did) and repent for your wrongdoings. To compensate today's mistakes, you should add some new measures for tomorrow in order to fill up those pits. One can't 'avoid' death, but one can do good deeds.

Mahaveer's voice, "You should be worried only for yourself. As everyone in this world is available to worry for the entire world, so except you no other person is going to worry about yourself." And the person here is literally dying by worrying about others. What will happen to my children? What will happen to my children's children? Do you think your grandchildren would be born deformed? You do not have to worry about who is going to take care of your business after you? Your business would be handled by your wife or children. You should worry for your bad days. Who will take care of you then?

Never sit idle. Always engage your mind and body in any honest work. An inactive man gets old very fast. When a man is tired and sits down, then ailments engulf him and such a man is rendered worthless for any work. If a man tires and sits down, then his fortune also sits down. Engage yourself in the acts of service even after you are retired from job. Do not rue over the memories of the past and let not the shadow of doubts about your future scare you; in fact, when you get up in the morning, do it with courage and think that 'today' is the only 'truth'.

It is easy to take out a strand of hair which is stuck in butter, but it is extremely difficult to take it out from a dried cake of a cow's dung. The soul which resides in the body of a saint is like the same strand of hair, stuck in butter. He lets go easily his soul at the time of death but the ignorant one cries at the time of his death because his soul is entangled in sexual desires, and these desires keep pulling him back into his family. Mother-sisters usually comment when a child is born, "Just look at the baby. Isn't he just like his grandfather?" He is not like his grandfather; he is grandpa himself who has come back in the form of a grandson.

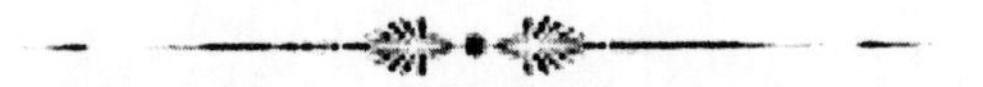

Jains have the exquisite merchandise of Mahaveer Swami in their possession, but its packing is inferior, whereas this era is of attractive packing. Jain community should either open the doors of its temples for the common people or take Mahaveer out from the walls of the temple and bring him to the town square for the benefit of the common man. When I say town square, I do not intend in any way to violate the boundaries of discipline or play with it. You will have to choose either one of the two. Either every common man should be given the right to go near Mahaveer or Mahaveer will have to reach every common man. What is your opinion?

Today's man has everything for his comfort and happiness. He has a TV-set, a DVD set, a diamond set, a tea set, a sofa set and many such sets. Only his 'mind' is 'upset', whereas everything else is set. His mind has become a university of complex thoughts and there is an endless turmoil of directionless thoughts in his mind. Everywhere there is tension. The remedy to tension is not 'medicine' but 'meditation'.

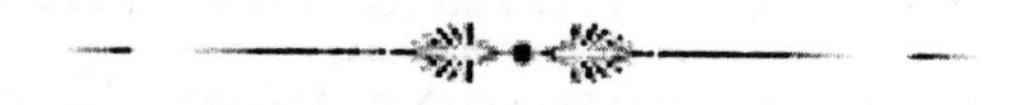

We must have a few critics also in our life. If there is no villain in the movie, then the personality of the hero does not shine. If we do not have a few critics, then we become careless. Critics keep us alert; where there are some pigs in the street, that street is always clean. Critics are like pigs who keep us pure. If someone starts criticizing, just think that stones are pelted only on that tree which bear sweet fruits. Only those people, who have some guts, are criticized in this world.

When you sit for your meal and if you find some flaws in the food, even then eat it as a blessing– 'Prasad'. Do not disturb your emotions. And yes, even if your emotions are disturbed do not let your language become abusive because if emotions are disturbed then only you will be hurt, but if your language deteriorates your entire family will be hurt. The language of anger is the expression of the Mahabharata. First feed the guest and only after that you should eat. What you eat would normally turn into waste but when the guest has eaten then your food transforms itself into 'Prasad', the blessings of the Lord.

Today life has become 'meaningless' due to loans and instalments. Till yesterday it was running 'smoothly', dependent on 'loan'. Buy any item on loan and spend rest of your life in repaying through instalments. Your house is now filled with gadgets like TV, fridge, washing machine, AC, car, computer, cell phone and what not. On enquiring– "Now enjoying?" They say, "No." "Then?" "Repaying through instalments." And in the process of repayment, this poor man ends up himself. Follow my advice to eat a simple meal, wear the simplest clothes, but do not go in for pomp and show by taking loans, end up paying more 'interest' than the 'principal'. Do remember, never underestimate anger, injury, fire and loan.

The wife asked, "What will you do if I die?" The husband replied, "How can this happen? I will never let you die." The wife replied, "That's all right; you can at least imagine what you will do if I die." The husband responded, "What will I do? I will just go mad." The wife asked, "Really?" The husband said, "Absolutely." The wife was overjoyed and asked, "That means you will not marry again." The husband smiled and said, "How can you predict a mad man's behavior? He can do anything." That is what the world is made up of.

Jain religion is the most mature and the greatest religion in the world, but its Jain followers are still immature to the tenets of this religion. Jain religion teaches 'Aparigraha'– non-possession, but the style is of 'Parigraha' *i.e.* accumulation. The culture of 'Shramana-tradition' (hard work) has become a 'Commercial-tradition'. Mahaveer himself stands naked, and it is very surprising that most of the cloth shops are run by the followers of Jainism. Mahaveer does not wear even a shred of cloth and the Jains are running 'Mahaveer Cloth Stores'. We are living a life of 'double-standard'. We consume liquor hideously and in public we even filter the water to drink it.

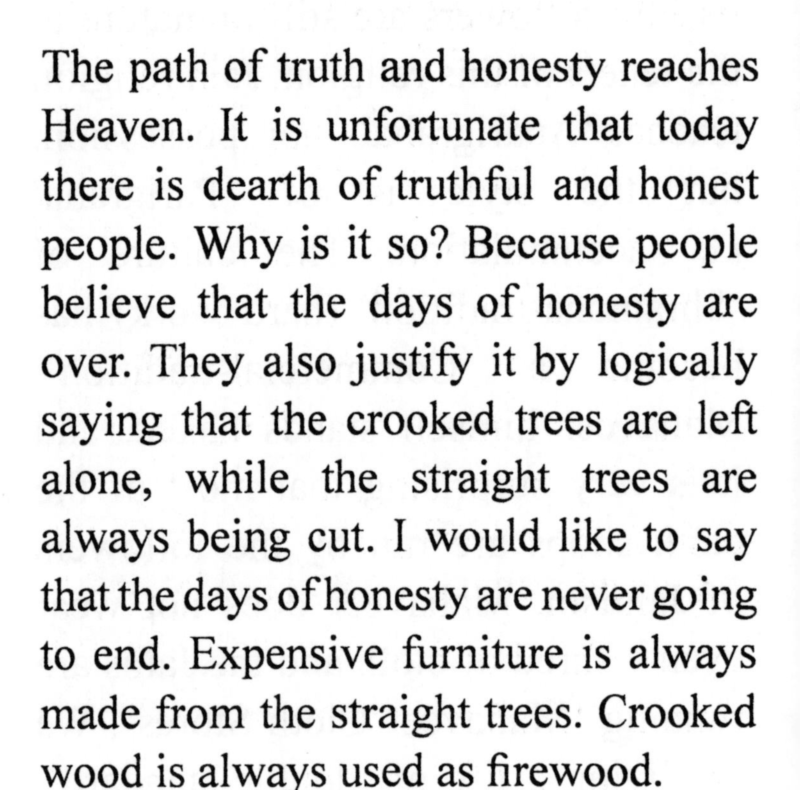

The path of truth and honesty reaches Heaven. It is unfortunate that today there is dearth of truthful and honest people. Why is it so? Because people believe that the days of honesty are over. They also justify it by logically saying that the crooked trees are left alone, while the straight trees are always being cut. I would like to say that the days of honesty are never going to end. Expensive furniture is always made from the straight trees. Crooked wood is always used as firewood.

Kind attention, senior citizens! Immediately stop getting angry, because nobody likes to see an elderly person in anger. It will be all right if the young display 'moderate anger', but the elderly should practise 'no anger' at all, not even 'moderate anger'. There is some value for your anger when you are young because you earn and support the family. They also tolerate your anger. But the one who does not earn, depends on someone for his livelihood and yet gets angry; he will not be liked. The value of the anger of an old man is like that of a dog. People say, "The old man has developed a habit of barking; let him bark."

If you have the attitude and the inclination to learn, then you can learn even from an ant, and if you don't have any inclination to learn, even Muni Tarunsagar cannot teach you. If you want to learn persistence and performance, learn it from an ant. An ant carries five times of its weight on its back and climbs the wall innumerable times, climbing & falling, but it does not lose courage. When it tries for the last time, it attains success. Do struggle, try hard; you are bound to achieve success. Everyone from Mahaveer to Mahatma Gandhi, the Buddha to Birla, Christ to Kiran Bedi, Adi Shankaracharya to Abdul Kalam and Tukaram to Tarunsagar had to struggle before they reached their goal.

There are three forms of a woman. They are Lakshmi– goddess of Wealth, Saraswati– goddess of Learning, Durga– goddess of Chivalry. To bring prosperity in the family, the woman should become Lakshmi. To educate her children, she should become Saraswati. To eradicate social evils, she should become Durga, riding on a lion. Women were strong in the past and it continues to be so even today. A man was grateful to her in the past and even today also he is grateful.

I asked a young man, “What do you do?” He said, “I study.” “Why do you study?” “To pass.” “Why do you want to pass?” “To get a certificate.” “Why do you want a certificate?” “To get a job.” “Why do you want a job?” “To earn money.” “Why do you want to earn money?” “To earn a livelihood.” “Why do you want to earn a livelihood?” “To live.” And at last, “Why do you want to live?” “I do not know.” This is a true fact with most of the people.

Two friends were talking; one of them said, "What sort of Kaliyug is this? It is dark everywhere. Between two dark nights there is only one bright day." Responding to this, the second friend said, "No, it is not so. There is only one dark night between two bright days." The circumstances are the same, but there is a vast difference between their viewpoints. What is your viewpoint?

Tears of a human being are rare. They are of three types. First– Tears of pain. If you shed tears after committing a sin, then these are the tears of pain. Second– Tears of loss. If you shed tears after losing someone, then these are the tears of loss. Third– Tears of gratitude if you shed tears while calling Him out of sheer devotion, then these are the tears of gratitude and greeting. Sati Chandana's tears were full of gratitude.

When a father cries, it means he has lost his successor. When the child cries, that means he has lost his support. If a sister cries, it means she has lost her festival of Rakshabandhan. If a wife cries, it means she has lost her husband. If a mother cries, it means she has lost her child who was her solace in her old age. If the whole village cries then it means that some saint has passed away and if some saints and sages also have tears in their eyes then you should understand that some Tirthankar has attained salvation. At the time of departure of Mahaveer Swami, there were tears in the eyes of Gautama as well.

Anger is not bad; if your tongue mingles with anger then it is bad. If the tongue were not to support anger, then the intensity of anger would have been null and if the anger gets the support of tongue then it leads to furious conflicts in life. Stop lending support of your tongue to your anger; I can guarrantee you that half of the conflicts in your life would end immediately. Anger is fire and you should become a water-current. Be an ocean of peace. Become Acharya Shantisagar.

You are the replica of a temple. When you sit cross-legged in Lotus Pose (Padmasana), then your expression and the profile is the replica of a temple. Your crossed legs are like the platform, your trunk is like a round sanctum sanatorium of the temple, your head is like a dome, your tuft is like a pitcher (kalash) and your ears and eyes resemble the windows. Your mouth is like a door, your soul is an idol and your mind is the priest, your body– temple is a seat of the formless Supreme Being. To recognize this Supreme Being is the installation of this body temple.

Once Gautama asked Mahaveer: "Bhantey! What is right– to give charity or to accumulate?" Mahaveer closed one of his fists and asked: "What would happen if this hand remains permanently like this?" Gautama said: "The hand would get stiff and ultimately render itself useless." Then Mahaveer opened the fist and asked: "What would happen if you keep the palm permanently like this?" "Even in this case the hand would become stiff and useless." Mahaveer said: "Gautama! It is important to open and close the fist in your life. It is important to earn and dispose of as well. What you consume might become useless but not what you give away.

It is good to do others' welfare, but it would be much better to find flaws in one's self. To speak the truth is good but to tell a lie to save someone's life is even better. If your character shines, it is good but if your love shines everywhere then it is much better. It is good to repay the loan but it is much better to carry out one's duty. To control evils is good while it is much better to invite good. It is 'good' to believe Tirthankars and their reincarnations but it is even 'better' to follow them.

An arrival of a saint is like an onset of spring. Nature smiles when spring arrives. When the saint arrives, culture smiles. The saint awakens the inner conscience of a man. He makes a man alert and stand up on his feet and enthuses energy in the standing man. To turn the dry leaves into greenery is the job of spring. To make a dead man alive is the job of a saint. 'Phalgun' brings the festival of flowers. Monsoon brings the dance of clouds. The saint brings gifts of joy. 'Nobody is stranger'– is the chant of religion. 'No other one'– is the mantra of love. 'No enmity'– is the mantra of saints.

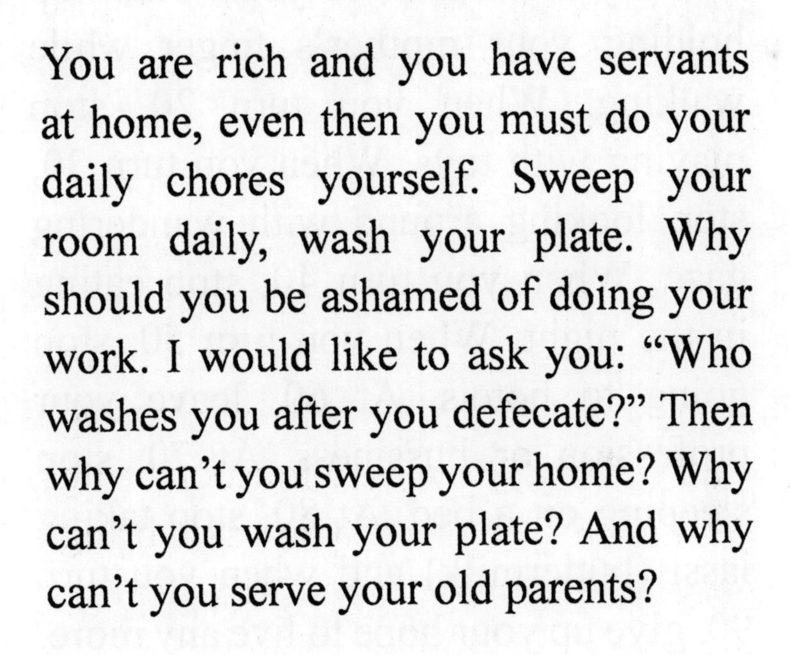

You are rich and you have servants at home, even then you must do your daily chores yourself. Sweep your room daily, wash your plate. Why should you be ashamed of doing your work. I would like to ask you: "Who washes you after you defecate?" Then why can't you sweep your home? Why can't you wash your plate? And why can't you serve your old parents?

When you become 10 years old, stop holding your mother's finger while walking. When you turn 20, stop playing with toys. When you turn 30, stop looking around with wandering gaze. When you turn 40, stop eating in the night. When you turn 50, stop going to hotels. At 60, leave your profession or bussiness. At 70, stop sleeping on a bed. At 80, stop taking lassi (buttermilk) and when you turn 90, give up your hope to live any more. On reaching 100, leave this world.

If you follow my advice then keep a garbage-bin in front of your house and put up a peg at your door. Why? When you return home from your shop, drop all the garbage of irritations in the bin and hang all your worries on the peg outside; then you enter your home smiling with a stress-free mind. It is evident that when you go to work, you are bound to face some difficulties, but why do your wife and children should suffer on account of this?

There are seven days from Monday to Sunday, but these seven days are of a week. I want to tell one more day, that is– Family day. Seven days make a week, 30 days make a month, and 12 months make a year. The same equation applies to the family as well. Today the meaning of family has become "we two, ours two". It doesn't include parents. Whereas the meaning of family is F-Father, A-and, M-Mother, I-I, L-Love, Y-You.

Today 'Satyam'-Truth and 'Shivam'-Purity are vanished from the trinity of 'Satyam-Shivam-Sundaram'(Truth, Purity and Beauty). Now, only 'Sundaram' is left. Today even the oldest man craves for the latest in fashion. Our society has mentioned sixteen types of 'Shringaar' (beautification) for ladies, but ever since 'Shringaar' has become a fashion, then onwards it has become commercial and gaudy. The difference between 'Shringaar' and 'Fashion' is as glaring as different between a fresh spring-water and bottled water. Clothes are also an important part of Shringaar. Clothes are meant to cover our bodies, but everyone knows that what kind of clothes are being worn today, just for fashion.

Nasruddin was going to Delhi. His friends told him, “Be careful; each item is quoted double its price there.” He reached Delhi. He went to a shop to buy an umbrella. He asked– “Brother! What is the price of this umbrella?” The shopkeeper said, “₹ 100.” Mulla remembered what his friends had told him– ‘Everything is quoted double its price’. He then offered ₹ 50. The shopkeeper said ₹ 80. Mulla said ₹ 40. The shopkeeper reduced it to ₹ 60. Mulla told, “₹ 30 only.” Now the shopkeeper got irritated and said angrily, “Take it free!” Mulla said– “Bade Miyan! then I will take two instead of one.” A man’s mind acts this way only.

There are some people who go to saints-munis and say: "Munishree! Please look into my hands." I tell them– "There is no need to show your palms. Just ask them to put their hands on your heads and bless you. Everything would fall in its place. Pray to their 'lotus feet' so that they may look at you with their 'lotus eyes' and would bless you with their 'lotus hands', and then your 'lotus faces' would be reflected joyfully."

These days, daughters are no less than sons in any way. They are boon to their parents. These days, they take better care of their parents than sons. In spite of staying in their in-laws' home, they take care of their parents, but sons do not take care of their parents even if they live with them. A daughter may tolerate anything being said to her in her in-law's home, but if anyone says anything against her parents, she would fiercely retaliate like 'the Queen of Jhansi' against 'Britishers'; whereas if the daughter-in-law abuses her in-laws in the presence of their son, the inept son doesn't even dare open his mouth.

तत्कालीन राष्ट्रपति डॉ. ए.पी.जे. अब्दुल कलाम,

22 जन. 2006, [illegible]मणबेलगोला

मुख्यमंत्री नरेन्द्र मोदी

29 अग. 2012, अहमदाबाद

मुनिश्री तरुणसागरजी : एक सफर

बाल्यकाल
1980

ब्रम्हचारी
1981

क्षुल्लक दीक्षा
1982

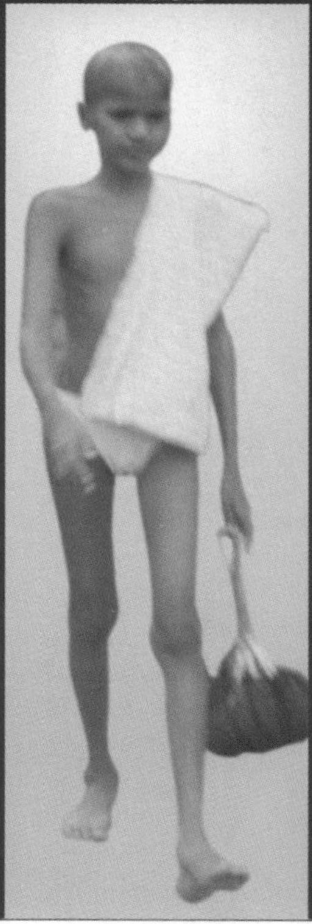

ऐलक दीक्षा
1984

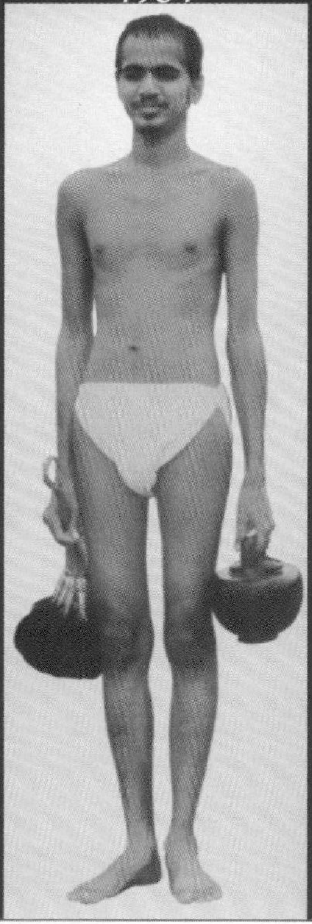

मुनि दीक्षा
1988

गुजरात प्रवेश
2 मार्च, 2003

गुजरात सरकार द्वारा 'राजकीय अतिथि' का सम्मान

Do not take any credit of doing something good. Give that credit to your parents, deity or Guru. By having that credit, you will bloat with ego. And if something goes wrong while accomplishing a task, take that responsibility. This will not only help you to correct the mistake but also get you protected from that sin. But you people are so dishonest that if the result is good you take all the credit and if the result is bad then you put the blame on others. Is this a justification?

There are three kinds of Laxmi (wealth). They are: Alaxmi– non-wealth, Laxmi– wealth and Mahalaxmi– enormous wealth. Wealth acquired by unethical means is Alaxmi. Wealth acquired by ethical means is Laxmi and wealth acquired with ethics, compassion and lawful norms is Mahalaxmi. Alaxmi brings disaster, Laxmi brings luxury and Mahalaxmi brings development. You can buy gold bangles for your wife through that wealth, which is unethical, but it is also likely that you may have to wear handcuffs for your unethical ways and means. Now tell what your viewpoint is.

If you pay heed to what Tarunsagar has to say, then I would like to request you to have purity in friendship and to have character because these are the real essence of life. As you know that due to bad company (friends) and vulgar photos, your character is going to be deteriorated. Bad friends and vulgar photos are lethal weapons which destroy your character. You can say they are a never-missing 'Brahmastra'.

If you suffer a loss in your business, do not burn your heart. Better think, you might have acquired some money by illegal means; it is good that it has gone by itself. If a cat drinks milk or a dog eats chapati, then think that it was meant for them only. If someone utters harsh words, do not feel bad. Think that he is an elderly fellow and, therefore, he has rebuked you for your own benefit as a well-wisher. If someone speaks ill of you, do not feel disheartened. If someone is angry, keep quiet. After shouting in anger for some time, he'll cool down by himself.

He who cares only for 'himself' is like Duryodhana, the one who cares for one's kith and kin is like Yudhishthir, and the one who cares for 'everyone' is like Shrikrishna. The one who cares only for oneself is a sinful soul, the one who cares for one's kith and kin is a noble soul, and the one who cares for everyone is a supreme soul. Duryodhana is a sinful soul, Yudhishthir is a noble soul, and Shrikrishna is a supreme soul. Now think who you are.

Do not let a saint and a soldier relax and sleep. If they go to 'sleep', then the future and destiny of the society and nation will also 'sleep'. Do not let a sinful person and a corrupt leader wake up, because if they get up, then the society and nation would lose their peace and happiness. If the saint and the soldier of a nation are alert and trustworthy, then such a nation can never be ruined. Only an alert saint and an honest soldier can ensure peace and prosperity for a nation.

I, Tarunsagar, do not advise you to run away from your family and profession. If you devote 23 hours and 55 minutes out of 24 hours of a day to your family and business, no problem at all, but spare at least 5 minutes for yourself. Also, spare some time for prayer and meditation. At the end of your life, you will find that you have been able to save only that time which you utilized on meditation; the rest has been lost.

A debate is going on, whether there is life on planet Mars or not, but nobody bothers whether there is auspiciousness (mangal) in your life. I would like to request that instead of searching for life on planet Mars (Mangal), it would be wise to search for auspiciousness (Mangal) in your life. Our life is auspicious, but due to our stupidity it has resulted into a 'wrestling bout'.

Wife and money are the means of devotion only, not of consumption. In a married life, if a man or woman is alone, then proper devotion cannot be completed. Both need each other. The relationship of the husband and the wife is meant for the devotion of the Supreme Being. Wealth is for service to mankind, not for consumption and merriment. If you get wealth due to the effect of your good deeds then you may engage servants for you, but never hire any servant for devotion to God, and to serve Guru and parents.

Mahaveer was immersed in meditation under a tree. The tree was laden with mangoes. Some children were also playing near by. They started pelting stones to get mangoes. One stone hit Mahaveer and it started bleeding from his head. The children got scared. They said: "Lord! Please forgive us, because we hurt you." The Lord said: "No, I am not hurt." They asked why you are crying. Mahaveer told: "You pelted stones at the tree and in turn it gave you sweet mangoes, but I could not give you anything in return. Therefore, I am sad."

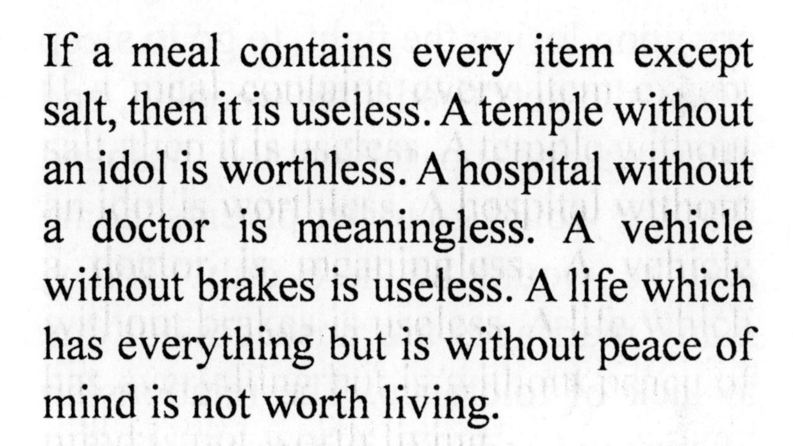

If a meal contains every item except salt, then it is useless. A temple without an idol is worthless. A hospital without a doctor is meaningless. A vehicle without brakes is useless. A life which has everything but is without peace of mind is not worth living.

Women have four habits: To fight, to cry upon losing the fight, to go to sleep when she gets tired after weeping, and after waking up telling the husband that she would go to her parents' home and he would be here only. Today, many marriages are unsuccessful due to lack of tolerance. The relationship of husband and wife is pure and divine, and it is based on 1- Trust, 2- Time, 3- Conversation and 4- Touch.

This world is not full of 'sorrow', but attachment to it brings sorrow. The house was on fire. The father started crying loudly. The neighbour said that his son had already sold the house on the previous day. The father stopped crying immediately. The son came running and said: "Father! The house is burning and what are you doing here?" Father said: "But you have already sold this house." The son said: "Yes, I was about to sell it but it is not yet sold off." The moment father heard this, he started crying bitterly again. Feeling of attachment always brings sorrow.

Foreign culture is based on the principle of 'Eating', 'Drinking' and 'Making Merry'. They live in a 'Hotel' and die in a 'Hospital', whereas the Indian culture subscribes that you should live in such a way that you may die in 'peace' and in a manner that everyone remembers you. The values in foreign culture teach us only 'learning' and 'earning' whereas values in Indian culture teach us 'living' also besides 'learning and earning'. Of the 72 Art forms in existence, 'Art of Living' is the most important.

Do not be afraid of problems. If you are scared of night, then you will never see dawn. Continue to move ahead with determination and strength. That's all! Dawn is about to break. Make your mind strong. You cannot accomplish anything with a weak mind. Remember, if you are feeling defeated in your mind, you are bound to lose and if you feel victorious in your mind, victory is yours. If you mentally lose the battle, the ship of your life is sure to sink and if you are strong-willed, you will conquer the world like Alexander.

The father thought of demonstrating to his son what poverty is. He went to his village along with his son. They lived among the poor for two days. After this, he asked him: "Son! What did you learn from the poor people in the village?" The son replied: "Father! We have one dog while they have four; they are richer than us. We buy everything from the market while they grow their grains, therefore they are richer than us. We cannot get good sleep even in an air-conditioned room while they can get sound sleep anywhere. They are really richer than us. Father! How glad I am that we came to this village! Otherwise, I would not have realised how poor we are."

There are four categories of people in this world. First– those who think that what belongs to them is already theirs and what belongs to others is also theirs. This is a false view. Second– those who think that what belongs to them is theirs and what belongs to others is not theirs. This is a balanced view. Third– those who think that what belongs to others is not theirs and what belongs to them is also not theirs. This is a saintly view. Fourth– those who think that nothing belongs either to them or to others. This is all a mess. This is the royal view– view of a swan. Which category do you belong to?

One day, you will be thrown out of the home, you built with your blood, sweat and toil. You will be sent out in a form of hearse. This Tarunsagar would like to request you that before you are driven out on a hearse, it is better that you should leave the home on your own on a pilgrimage with a 'Kamandal' and a 'picchi' or submit yourself to the service of some saint. So, what is your view?

There are many types of anger. First is– 'Extreme anger' which is like a line drawn on a stone. Second is– 'Huge anger' which is like a line drawn on a brick. The third is– 'Slight anger' which is like a line drawn on sand and the last and fourth is 'Sweet anger' which is like a line drawn on the surface of water which is just momentary. Only 'Slight anger' and 'Sweet anger' are acceptable in normal family life. 'Extreme anger' and 'Huge anger' have to be given up under any circumstances.

There is a narrow street. Suppose, a king is passing through it and all of a sudden if he is confronted by a raging bull then what should he do? Should he say to the bull, "O Bull, you must get out of my way because I am the king." The bull is likely to say: "If you are the king, I am the emperor. Come on; face me." It would be only wise if the king finds a raised platform near by and climbs on it or retrace his steps. We meet many such bulls every day, but we must not confront with them, because confrontation is the cause of attrition and shattering.

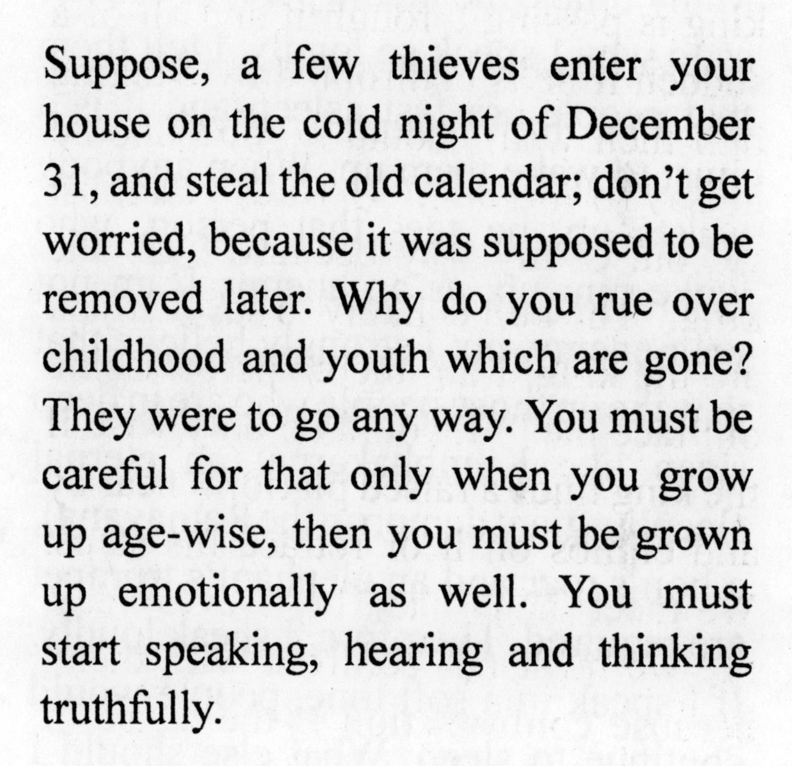

Suppose, a few thieves enter your house on the cold night of December 31, and steal the old calendar; don't get worried, because it was supposed to be removed later. Why do you rue over childhood and youth which are gone? They were to go any way. You must be careful for that only when you grow up age-wise, then you must be grown up emotionally as well. You must start speaking, hearing and thinking truthfully.

Many times, the media persons ask me as to why I speak so loudly. I tell them that people are fast asleep and it is a must to wake them up. When anybody wakes up, he sees that person, who woke him up, as an enemy. I am not your enemy, but I strongly believe that to wake up those people who are in deep sleep like Kumbhakarna (an eternal sleeping giant demon in the Ramayana), a lion's roar and an elephant's trumpet are required. Therefore, I speak loudly. If I speak in a soft tone, people would continue to sleep. What else should I do?

I do not give any false assurance to anyone, because false assurance may become a cause of worry at any time. I do not wish to live in a state of uncertainty nor do I keep my audience in a state of confusion and uncertainty. I only tell the bitter facts of life because someone has to take an initiative to show a person his real face at some time or the other. I always think why I shouldn't show them the reality and when they confront the reality, they comment that Munishree uses bitter words and delivers bitter discourses. I do not relish delivering bitter discourses; I am bound to do it because of my commitment and sense of duty.

I was in Kothli town. I was proceeding towards the venue of discourse when I saw a few people were also travelling towards the venue in a car very speedily. A rich man passed by me in a Mercedes car. I said to him, "O rich man! You have a Mercedes car while I have a Namo kar (Holy chant). Your Mercedes car can ditch you at any time but my Namo kar wouldn't." Yes! There is one similarity between a car and Namo kar. A car is of no use without petrol and Namo kar is also useless without devotion and faith.

A Saint and the Sun never stay at one place, and wherever they go they alleviate darkness and spread light. A Saint is like flowing water and blowing air. A Saint is like fragrance. Air spreads fragrance. A devotee does the job of spreading his saint's greatness. A Saint is the beginning of a new dawn and he always gets engrossed in meditation. Those, who do not meditate, are simply a crowd of belly-filling animals.

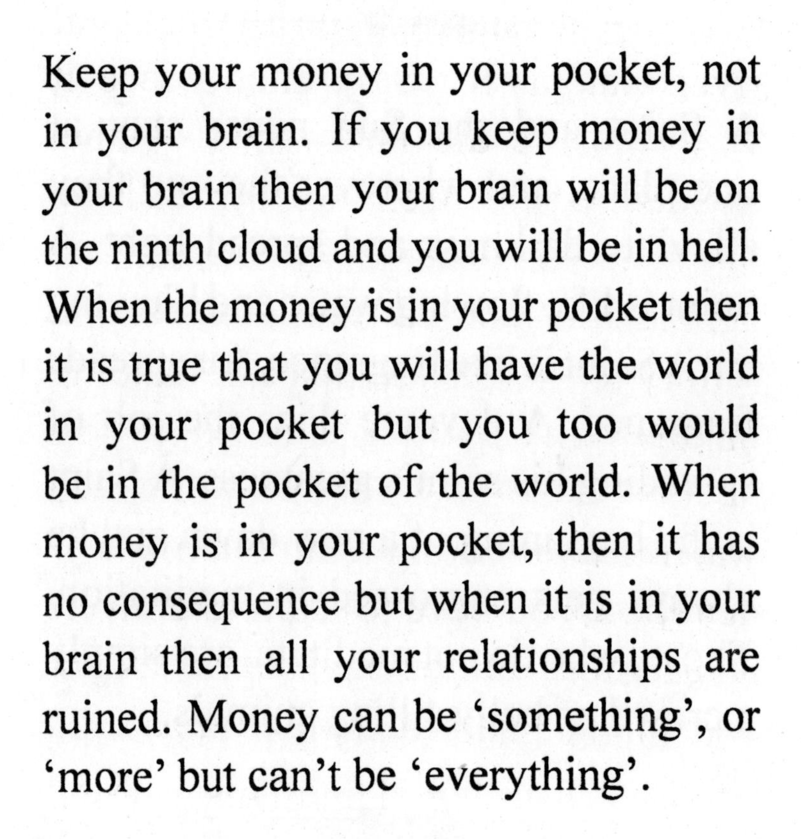

Keep your money in your pocket, not in your brain. If you keep money in your brain then your brain will be on the ninth cloud and you will be in hell. When the money is in your pocket then it is true that you will have the world in your pocket but you too would be in the pocket of the world. When money is in your pocket, then it has no consequence but when it is in your brain then all your relationships are ruined. Money can be 'something', or 'more' but can't be 'everything'.

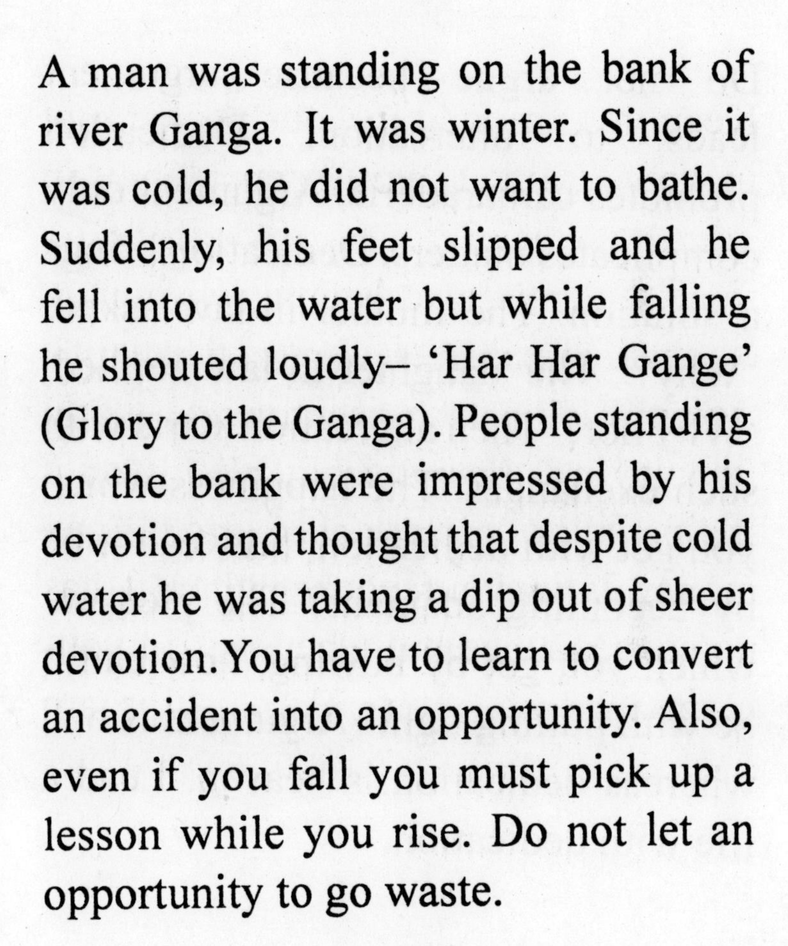

A man was standing on the bank of river Ganga. It was winter. Since it was cold, he did not want to bathe. Suddenly, his feet slipped and he fell into the water but while falling he shouted loudly– 'Har Har Gange' (Glory to the Ganga). People standing on the bank were impressed by his devotion and thought that despite cold water he was taking a dip out of sheer devotion. You have to learn to convert an accident into an opportunity. Also, even if you fall you must pick up a lesson while you rise. Do not let an opportunity to go waste.

Do not argue because argument leads to altercation. Dedication promotes camaraderie. Argument only complicates matters. Dedication brings a solution. The mother-in-law asked, 'Why?' The daughter-in-law replied, 'Why not?' Then altercation starts with such exchanges. The happiness which you get with dedication, how can it be by becoming adamant? The pleasure which you get by bowing, how can it be with pulling tight? Argument is hell whereas dedication is heaven. Lead a life with dedication.

You do not own anything other than your own self here. Nobody can snatch away what you have and you cannot snatch anything from others which really does not belong to you. Remember one thing: You are only 'you'.There is nobody in this world who is exactly like you. The lines on your thumb do not match with those of any other thumb and that is why thumb impression is taken as your signature.

Begin your day with cheerfulness and greetings. A man who gets up and smiles even for a minute, he gets a power-tonic for the whole day and a person who kneels down before his parents, teacher and God does not have to kneel down before anybody in his entire life. A person who has the treasure of good wishes is rich in true sense. He becomes wealthy and prosperous with this wealth only.

I spoke very sweetly in the first ten years of my sainthood but it used to put people to sleep. During those days, hardly 25 - 50 people used to attend my discourses. Those 25 - 50 people were either driven out of their homes by their daughters-in-law or were not allowed in their shops by their sons. They would come and sleep during my discourses. I used to feel very bad. When I asked them if they were sleeping, they would deny it and I would feel cheated. Then I would ask if they were awake, they would deny this too. After that only, situation used to become clear and favourable.

How long can you keep a spring pressed? Here 'Spring' is related to 'Mind'. Your mind is also like a spring. It is very fickle and restless. It can't stick at one place and swings like a pendulum. While your body is in one place, the mind may have gone somewhere else! Your body is physically present in a temple but your mind may be wandering in the kitchen. It would be better if mind visits a temple to seek His blessings but it has made the temple as a 'wrestling arena'.

A saint is the one who befriends the poor, the illiterate and the exploited because they are closest to God. Our country is facing the problem of 'Inequality' not 'Poverty'. If the entire wealth of a nation of 120 crore is in the hands of just 200 to 300 families, then it is bound to be trapped in poverty. Our country is a land of gold (a golden sparrow), then how can it be poor?

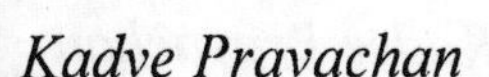

Non-violence is the first entrance to religion and a great celebration of amity. Violence can never be a part of any religion even if it is committed in the name of any god or goddess. Non-violence and truth have been the most supreme principles of our country. Our national emblem also has 'Satyameva Jayate' (Truth always wins) inscribed on it. I strongly believe that as long as we see tears in the eyes of a human being or an animal, these principles of non-violence and truth are futile and incomplete. We must put in all efforts to promote these principles.

Offerings through your hands is called sacrifice and offerings through your heart is Vairagya (dispassion or detachment). Vairagya is much more than sacrifice. The one who is engaged in caring for his body, for him wealth is a mortal being while someone who is engaged in caring for his mind for him life is a saint. You can sacrifice your body and wealth for your family. No need to worry. But give your mind to your god only. If you surrender your mind to the world then you will have to repent. Let Him be the only master of your mind.

Meera was immersed in her devotion and was singing a 'Bhajan'. One expert musician too was sitting in the court. As per him, the co-ordination between rhythm and tune was not proper, so he wrote on the wall– 'To sing in a melodious mode.' Meera came out of her reverie. She completed her devotional song. When she saw what was written on the wall, she added one more word to that line- Sing with fondness. When you sing in a melodious mode, the world around you is happy whereas if you sing with fondness, then God becomes happy. What do you want? You have to decide yourself.

Whatever be the sorrows and hardships come in your life, do not give up worship. Do you give up eating when you face difficulties? Do you stop breathing when you fall sick? Not at all. Then, why do you stop your worship? Never give up, at least, these two things- devotional song and food. If you give up food, you will be no more. If you stop singing devotional song then you will not stand anywhere. In true sense, 'A devotional song itself is food'. As a matter of fact, prayer itself is food.

If your clothes get soiled, you wash them with soap; if your mind gets dirty then what will you do? To cleanse your mind, you should be in the company of pious people (Satsang). Your mind is cleansed with the soap of Satsang. When people go to the temple, they usually change their clothes and wear clean and neat clothes. But I would like to tell you that you should go not only in clean clothes but also you should change your mind, have clean thoughts. The reason is that He does not look at your clothes; He just wants to see your clean and pure heart.

There should be a proper coordination between the vocalist & the instrumentalist. When there is harmony between the two, the music would be full of sweetness and melody. If there is no harmony, it would become cacophonous. For a happy married life, the husband and the wife must have coordination and understanding between them. There has to be consistency of each other's nature, thoughts and likes and dislikes. If they are at loggerheads, quarrels are imminent. Their nature should be like water which can be mixed up anywhere very easily.

A saint asked a man time. That man was of vile nature. He hit on the saint's head with a staff and told, "Baba! It's one o' clock." Instead of feeling sad, the saint felt very happy and started dancing with joy. Someone asked, "Baba! Are you mad? He hit you and you are dancing, why?" The saint said that he was thanking God because he did not ask for time an hour back; otherwise, he would have been struck 12 times. If you decide to be happy under any circumstances, then nobody can hurt you.

A true devotee does not care for the world. He does not worry about what the world thinks about him, speaks about him, etc. All that he says to Him is, 'O God! Whatever you do, I'll enjoy that.' Worldly acts and devotion can never go hand in hand. The world finds comfort in materialistic things while a devotee lives in meditation. Someone living in a materialistic world gets death while a person who lives in meditation attains salvation.

Make mistakes– may be once, twice or even thrice, but make sure not to commit the same mistake again. Only those people who make attempts to achieve something make mistakes. Only those people fall who walk. Learn from your mistakes. It is the biggest impunity not to learn from mistakes. Even if you fall, bounce back like a ball. Do not fall like a lump of clay which falls and gets stuck there. Do not repeat the mistake in the morning; if at all you have to repeat it, do it in the afternoon.

Nature has arranged the system in such a way that you cannot choose your parents, but you can, at least, choose your friends. He who teaches you bad habits gets you addicted and betrays you in your bad times; he cannot be your true friend. He who protects you teaches you good things and takes care of you; he is a true friend. He uses harsh & bitter words, even though he is your ture friend. I, Muni Tarunsagar, will never pat you on your back. In fact, if you come to me, you are most certain to be rebuked.

Life is a battlefield. All of you are warriors. Everyone has to fight with life here. You face problems in life. Learn to confront with them. You cannot afford to bend before them or kneel down. Challenges in life are also like an election. You will have to face the election. There is no escape. This is a courageous act like jumping from a plane with a parachute. You will have to come out from this vicious circle of hopelessness; you can't do anything. You cannot say that you are helpless.

Anger is the biggest enemy of a human being and if you are possessed by it, then it will come out only when you become bankrupt. Where there is anger, how can you expect Diwali! There would be only bankruptcy. Every angry person has to pay the price for his anger some day. Therefore, do not get angry every day, only once a week. If you get angry just for a while then its effect would be there. If you get angry very often in a day then people would say you have no other work and have developed this habit of getting angry anytime.

Those who do not have to swallow a pill in order to go to sleep and an alarm to wake up are the happiest people in this world. The one who carries out his duty diligently but not a borrower is a happy man today. The one who has strong faith in his hard work and smiles in every circumstance is a happy man. These days, people hire a servant for everything: to fetch you drinking water, to cook, to sweep and to clean the house and for every other conceivable work. Even people hire servants to take care of their old parents. I am worried if in future, you have to hire a servant to love your wife too.

There are different categories of thieves. The ones– who break the lock and steal, who shy away from work but earn a huge profit by unethical means, who do not feed their guest first and eat, who do not part with what rightfully belongs to others, who do not take care of their parents, who do not give alms to the beggar who comes to their doorstep, who enjoy a lot without doing any work, and those husbands, sons and fathers who do not do their duties can also be called thieves. Now tell me into which category you fall.

Never allow your mind to get weakened. Do not lose courage. It does not matter much if your body is weak but your mind should be strong. However, if your mind is weak and body is strong then it will not work out. You will have to face numerous challenges in your life. Everyone from Kalidas, Tulsidas to Kabirdas had to face challenges and passed through many ordeals. You too will have to face them. Nature has brought us into this world to contribute something good; therefore, never let your mind to get weakened. Have strong faith. Do not lose heart if you do not have shoes and you have to walk barefoot, because there are thousands of people who do not have even feet.

Make your children strong like a jungle-plant, not like a protected plant in a pot, so that even if nobody waters them, they may bloom with their inner strength. Children should not learn through teaching, rather, they should learn through observation. The children who are set free from the slavery of a clock and calendar will be successful in their life. 'A line of Control' is necessary in life to become successful. However high you may raise in position in your life, do not abandon your religion.

Everyone is only a thief in this world. Some are inexperienced while the others are experienced. The one who is caught while stealing is an inexperienced person and the one who steals with such finesse that he is not caught is a seasoned person. People who indulge in major crimes have become big industrialists whereas petty thieves become small shopkeepers and businessmen. Those who did not get an opportunity to cheat and steal became the so-called honest people. Today, our honesty is also by default and compulsion, as we didn't get any opportunity for dishonesty.

The foundation of husband-wife relationship is mutual trust. In fact, every relation stands on the foundation of trust, but in this relationship trust is on the top. This relationship cannot last without this trust and mirrors cannot be sold off in the city of the blind. The importance of trust is as high as breathing to stay alive. One cannot survive without breathing and relationships cannot last without mutual trust and understanding.

Religion and youth are two sides of the same coin. Mahaveer is the first philosopher in the world who associated religion with the youth because energy is required for religion and youth is the treasure of energy for religion. Religion is not a medicine for the old; it is a tonic to become young. If you reverse the word 'Youth' in Hindi (Yuva– Vayu) then youth is dynamic like Vayu– the wind or air. A river and air do not expect respite or rest. Also, the Sun does not expect anything. Similarly, there is nothing impossible for youth.

One gentleman was saying to me that he couldn't get rid of anger. What should he do for this? He was feeling helpless. I told him not to worry. I asked him to give ₹100 to his servant every time whenever he would get angry. If he got angry twenty times in a day, he would calculate in the night as to how much money he had given to the servant. Next day, he should try to reduce the sum to ₹1500 and then try hard to bring this sum down to ₹100. When you realise that it needs a lot of hard work to earn even ₹100 then you may not want to lose that too. Do remember-Anger is a costly affair.

Once a king fell ill. All the treatments proved an exercise in futility. Someone advised that the king should be made to wear the clothes of someone who is happy in every aspect. He would then be cured. The soldiers went in all the directions in search of such a person, but wherever they went they were disappointed. Because everyone was sad for one or the other reason. One day, the minister saw a person, at a distance, who was glowing with joy and happiness. He seemed to be the happiest man on the earth, but when the person came near to him, he was shocked. He was none other than a Digambar Muni.

Truth is of two categories– Practical truth and Absolute truth. The fact that your wife, children, house and shop belong to you is a practical truth while the Absolute truth is that even your own body doesn't belong to you. Alexander the Great had experienced the Absolute truth during the last few moments of his life. He instructed his men to keep his hands outside the carriage during the funeral procession so that the world might see that though Alexander amassed a lot of riches yet he left this world empty-handed.

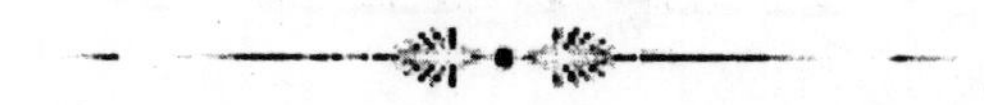

Nothing is impossible for you. Why do you think that you would not be able to accomplish this? I say there is nothing in the world which you cannot accomplish. Please put a 'full stop' to such negative thoughts today itself. Do it here and now, and before you go to bed every night and when you get up in the morning, take a vow that 'I can, I must and I will'. Make this sentence your ideal and motto in your life and surge ahead with this confidence that there is nothing beyond your reach.

There was a lazy man. He was resting around happily in his farm. Someone asked him, "Brother! Why don't you do farming?" This lazy man asked him what would happen if he worked. His well-wisher said, "You would reap a good harvest and you could earn a lot of money." The lazy man asked what would happen if he earned more. The well-wisher said he could have a family and a home. The lazy man repeated what would happen then. The wise man said that he could live in comfort. The lazy man just turned and retorted– "What am I doing right now?" Due to such lazy idiots and half dead people in the society, the country would never see good days.

You might have fought with your husband many times. Now get into a fight one more time on my request. If your husband drinks, chews tobacco, smokes or gambles, tell him very clearly that he must give up these vices, otherwise, either he or you would stay in the house. Adopt such a method by which you can improve him because you are his better half and you are entitled to this title when you show him the right path and help him to tread on this path.

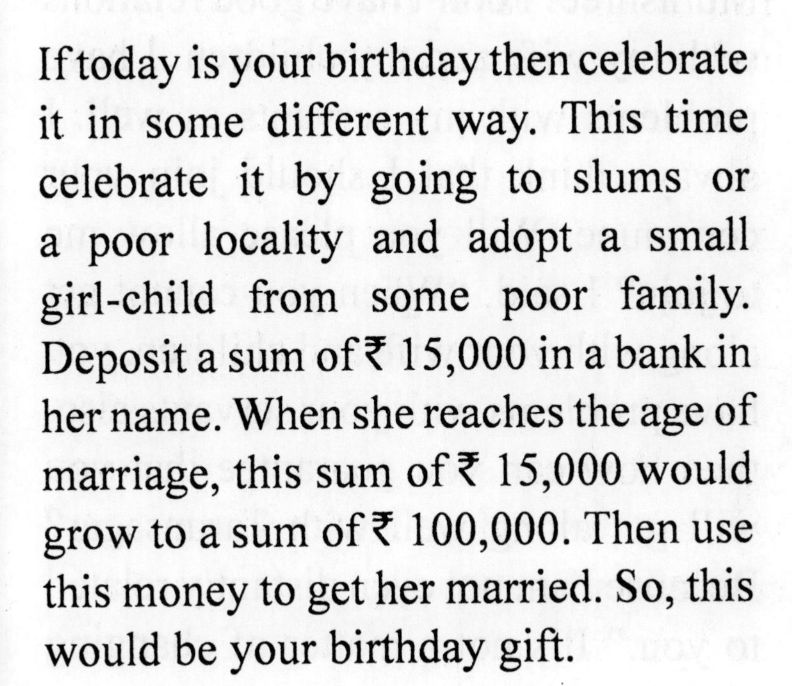

If today is your birthday then celebrate it in some different way. This time celebrate it by going to slums or a poor locality and adopt a small girl-child from some poor family. Deposit a sum of ₹ 15,000 in a bank in her name. When she reaches the age of marriage, this sum of ₹ 15,000 would grow to a sum of ₹ 100,000. Then use this money to get her married. So, this would be your birthday gift.

Munishree! I don't have good relations with my wife and my children. I have problems with my servants as well. I always think that I should join your commune. Will you please allow me to join? I said, "When you cannot get along with your wife and children, you have problems with your servants also, then how can you guarantee that you will get along well with Tarunsagar? Because I am not even distantly related to you." It's not a matter of changing place; you have to change your nature.

The daughter-in-law was British. She did not know Hindi. One day, her mother-in-law called her maid as 'gadhi' (she donkey). The daughter-in-law asked her husband the meaning of 'gadhi'. The husband told her that it means 'moti' (fat). Next day, the mother-in-law rebuked her maid again and called her 'ullu ki patthi (like an owl). The daughter-in-law again asked her husband the meaning of this term. To get rid of his wife, her husband told her it means 'dubli patli' (thin). After some days, the mother-in-law fell ill. The daughter-in-law looked at her mother-in-law and said, "Hey Mom! A few days back you were so 'gadhi' (fat) and now you have become absolutely 'ullu ki patthi'." Reap as you sow!!

It is said that there is no remedy for suspicion. It's true that even legendary Hakeem Lukman did not have a cure for suspicion. Once the thought of suspicion enters the mind, it continues to stay and it comes out only after eroding the brain. The wife of a person was very suspicious by nature. One day, she started looking for long hair on the coat of her husband. When she did not find any hair on the coat, she said to her husband, "Excellent! Now you are doing romance with a bald lady. Truly! There is no remedy for suspicion."

If you want to be happy in your life, learn to make 'adjustments'. The one who cannot make adjustments according to the surrounding circumstances, is rejected everywhere. You cannot get everything in this world which suits your likes and dislikes. A few things may be suitable for others and not for you and therefore be prepared for such situations as well. Mould yourself as per the circumstances. This is the secret of happy life. The one who cannot adopt himself according to the changed circumstances, has no other option; else he should commit suicide.

It's a matter of great pride to have parents in a person's life. The responsibility of the parents towards their children is far more than that of our Prime minister towards his citizens. If the parents do not give proper respect to their aged parents then they also do not have any right to expect any respect from their children. Do not have too much attachment and affection towards your children because one day they may even become your neighbours. You should be their trustee rather than be the owner. If they do not listen to you then you need not tell them again and again. They would automatically learn when they suffer a kick of adversity.

You must appreciate the fact that money is a path, not the destination. Money is only money, not your master. It is ‘something’, can be ‘even more’ but it cannot be ‘everything’. Those who think money is everything have to repent in the end. Blood and money are almost similar. Both must keep on flowing. Some people are the masters of their wealth while some are the servants of their wealth. What about you?

Always remember– Whatever you give that only comes back to you and in multifold. Every farmer knows this rule, accepts it and works on it. He sows excellent seeds in his farm and sees the results. He waits for the crop. This world is like an echo, so whatever you give, only that would come back. Flowers give flowers and thorns come back as thorns. By gathering only you can't survive, so whatever you want, then start distributing that only.

The home of a married person is his place of enjoyment. The house is full with the atoms of desires and they keep having evil influence on your mind. Therefore, leave your home just for one month in a year. Go on a pilgrimage and pray there. You will get mental peace. I believe that the condition of the house improves when you leave it. Do not forget that one day you have to leave the house or bungalow or the palace you live in.

Do not forget that one day you have to leave this world without taking anything with you. When you die, your servants will stand by with both palms joined in reverence, your 'iron safe' will lie at the same place and your palatial home too will not change its position. Your wife would cry too much and accompany you till the end of your street and your pall bearers would be in a hurry because some of them have to open their shops while someone else has to go to office. They would insist on putting more firewood to engulf your corpse as fast as possible. You may find a large number of people to accompany you till the funeral pyre, but after that only your good deeds and sins would accompany you on your later journey.

Our sisters are also hot-headed. They fight with their mothers-in-law but spurt out their anger on their children. But I strongly believe that fights can be resolved through mutual understanding. Once a couple started arguing. The quarrel got aggravated to such an extent that the wife got upset and said to her husband that he had to take care of his house and she would be leaving for her parents' home. Her husband assumed serious proportions of that situation. The husband changed his demeanour and said, "OK, you may go to your parents' home. I would also visit my in-laws' house and children would also visit their maternal grandparents' house and would have a nice stay there."

In our marriages, there is a tradition to go around a holy fire for seven times. The bride and the bridegroom go around seven times and take a vow to lead a life of faith and servitude with each other. I believe that there should be an eighth round too. This should be to prevent foeticide (infant's killing). The bride and the bridegroom should vow that they would never commit the heinous act of foeticide. So long as the birth of a girl-child is not welcomed and not treated as a joyous event like on the arrival of a boy, till then we have to accept that our Indian society is guilty of being biased towards boys.

If you are a mother-in-law then you must give so much love to your daughter-in-law that she should forget her parents' home and even their phone number as well. And if you are a bride then after attending and listening to my discourse, your dressing table should have very less number of cosmetics. If you are a son then you should lead such an ideal life that the whole world would ask your parents about their good deeds by virtue of which they have such a wonderful son like you, and if you are a father then you will have to instil such faith in your grown-up son's mind with your behaviour that he need not wait for his father's death to get the keys of the iron safe.

Anger is like fire, which is very dangerous. You do not know when the fire of anger would spread and its leaping flames would engulf the joys of the family and burn them one by one. Therefore, always have some water in the house; here water means 'forgiveness' and 'tolerance'. Adopt compassion within yourself and have patience. There is no dearth of advisors but there is paucity of tolerance. If you do not have the capacity to tolerate, then your home would witness quarrels and turmoil daily. Here one has to digest the dung of abuses and insults, and you can't expect sweet praising words every time.

I would like to ask you a question– What do you know about 'mukhagni?' You would say that when a person dies, then the flame which ignites the funeral pyre is called 'mukhagni', but I would say, that is not 'mukhagni'; rather, that is 'chitagni'. Do you know? The real 'mukhagni' is that when a person smokes bidi-cigarette. That person, who is puffing, is igniting his own funeral pyre while he is alive.

Today's man, although is living in an air-conditioned room, yet he has a heater switched on in his brain. If you want to be successful in life, have an 'ice factory' in your head and a 'sugar factory' in your mouth. If a person gets rid of the heat from his brain and has softness in his tongue then your family is going to be well-off. One question, when do you get angry? You are angry when your expectations turn sour resulting into frustration. Therefore, do not expect anything; then you do not have to confront the peril of frustration and neglect. Be careful: a minute's anger is enough for ruining your entire future.

Bharat had gone to the forest, in order to convince Rama to return to Ayodhya. He crossed the Ganga on the way. Everyone bathed in the Ganga and when they crossed the Yamuna, they bathed in the Yamuna too. In the end, they came across the Saraswati but everyone except Bharat bathed in the Saraswati. People asked him: "O King! Why didn't you bathe in the Saraswati?" Bharat replied, "I will not bathe in this river because this river gave ill-conceived advice to my mother to send my elder brother Rama into exile." When he reached Rama, he asked Bharat, "Yes Bharat! Which position do you wish to occupy?" Bharat said, "My Lord! I do not want any position but your wooden sandals. The one, who is successful in acquiring Thy feet, will conquer the world in any case."

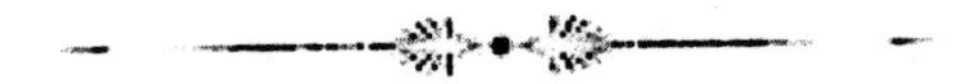

Always remember my three points for a happy life. First: You should be able to live in a proper manner, Second: You should be able to express yourself properly and Third: You should have the patience to bear pain at the time of crisis. We are unable to live properly. We cannot express ourselves properly and, in fact, we have no tolerance at all. When the parents try to say something to their children, the kids do not tolerate the words of their parents and run away from home.

People are ignorant and have blind faith. They sacrifice animals before deities in the name of religion. They defend themselves by saying that Mother goddess had also killed Mahishasur. But they should know that Mother goddess had killed a demon by the name of Mahish and here you are killing an animal Mahish (a buffalo). You are sacrificing goats. You should feel ashamed of killing these innocent and dumb animals. Do remember– They may be dumb but they have life. Which mother would be happy to see her kids getting killed?

It is said that even Nature does not like anyone to utter bitter words. That's why the tongue does not have a bone. Although there is not even a single bone in your tongue yet it gets annoyed and is capable enough of breaking all the bones of body. Therefore speak less and only that which is worth. It should soothe the mind. Always speak softly and sweetly. Tarunsagar Ji alone is sufficient to utter bitter words. You should not speak bitter.

If you wear an expensive watch, the world will move around you. But in your difficult time, only God would be your saviour. When you face any problem in your life, you must not knock at the door of your friend; you may unhesitatingly knock at His door any time because this mortal life is fake. Nobody would help you in your hour of need. As long as things are rosy, everyone would be yours. Even a bird also hides in the nest at the time of dusk.

A Jain community is more happier and prosperous than other sects. Why? Because this sect abstains from bad habits. That is why it is happy and prosperous. This sect is taught right from childhood to abstain from wine, meat, smoking, gambling, and to have control over eating habits. In the absence of these bad habits, they can easily save a lot of money and this saving makes them happy and prosperous.

I do not speak those words which are full of flattery and going to please you. I always speak harsh truth. Truth is always bitter. It is not in my nature to say bitter things; it is my compulsion. My discourses are not lullabies which 'lull' you into sleep but these are 'slaps' in your face which make you awake. A lullaby cannot wake up the society, which is in deep slumber. If anybody says bitter words, which are beneficial to you, then listen to them because this would not only make him happy but also bring joy to his life.

Sometimes people talk unnecessary and fight without any reason. For ex: A husband and a wife had a conflict over their son. The husband was saying: "I want to make him an engineer." The wife was saying: "No, I will make him a doctor." They both started fighting. In the meantime, their neighbour came and advised: "Why don't you ask your son what he wants to be." Hearing this, the husband and the wife smiled and said, "Our son is not yet born." So, most of our fights are baseless. The formula of a happy life is-'Speak less, speak worthwhile.'

A smile is the biggest 'Invitation card' in the world. If you want to love someone or you want to endear yourself to all, then always smile. Smile does not have any side-effects. You must notice that even an old man looks better when he smiles, and even a child looks ugly when he cries. It is only a human being who can smile. Have you ever seen an animal smiling?

How the time has changed! There was a time when a guard used to sit to prevent a dog entering into the house and now a dog sits at the door to prevent a man from entering into the house. In the olden times, during a marriage, our womenfolk used to cook the food and hired women used to dance; now the hired women cook the food while the household women dance. It is now, almost, reversed.

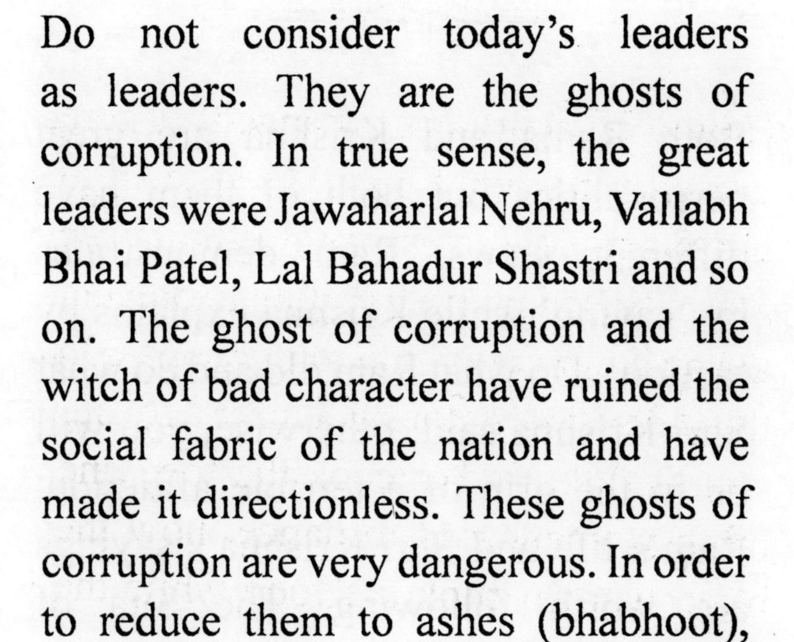

Do not consider today's leaders as leaders. They are the ghosts of corruption. In true sense, the great leaders were Jawaharlal Nehru, Vallabh Bhai Patel, Lal Bahadur Shastri and so on. The ghost of corruption and the witch of bad character have ruined the social fabric of the nation and have made it directionless. These ghosts of corruption are very dangerous. In order to reduce them to ashes (bhabhoot), we need a great soul (avadhoot) like Mahatma Gandhi.

Both Rama and Krishna are great personalities but both of them have different views. Ram demonstrates by 'saying' while Krishna explains by 'action'. Do what Ram did and do what Shri Krishna said; otherwise, you will be in the grip of a terrible affliction. Ram's life and Shri Krishna's sayings are worth following. The Sita of the Ramayana and the Geeta of the Mahabharata are the cultures of this country.

Five tasks are very difficult in this world. First, to push an elephant over. Second, to catch a giraffe's neck. Third, to massage a mosquito. Fourth, to kiss an ant. Fifth, to smile after getting married. The first four points are OK but the fifth one, which is about marriage and smile, is difficult. What is the relationship between marriage and smile? This is like smiling and puffing your cheeks at the same time. The occasion was the bride's departure from her parents' house. The bride was weeping while the bridegroom was smiling. Probably the bride was 'weeping' for the last time and the bridegroom was 'smiling' for the last time.

Philosophers called the mirage of life as a dancer (Nartaki). She makes the soul to wander in 84 lakh births. It keeps the married men entangled in worldly pleasures of body and keeps the saints engrossed in reputation and fame. When we read the letters (in Hindi) in 'Nartaki' backwards, it becomes 'Kirtan'. It means you must engage in the Kirtan of Lord so that the Nartaki may not hurt you in any way and you remain unscathed.

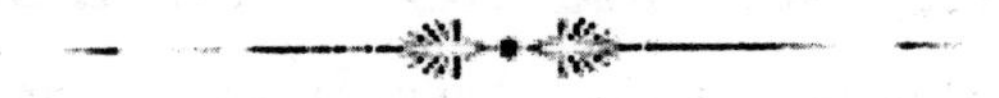

Once number 9 slapped number 8. Number 8 started crying. Number 9 said: I am bigger, so I hit you. When he heard this, number 8 hit number 7 and he repeated what number 9 had said and this went on. Like number 7 hit 6 …….. and ultimately 2 hit number 1. Now whom could number 1 hit? It had 0 before it. 1 did not hit number 0; instead, lifted it with affection and placed near him. Immedietely, after that, number 1 grew in power; it became 10 times. Pardon brings glory to the brave (Kshma Veerasya Bhushnam).

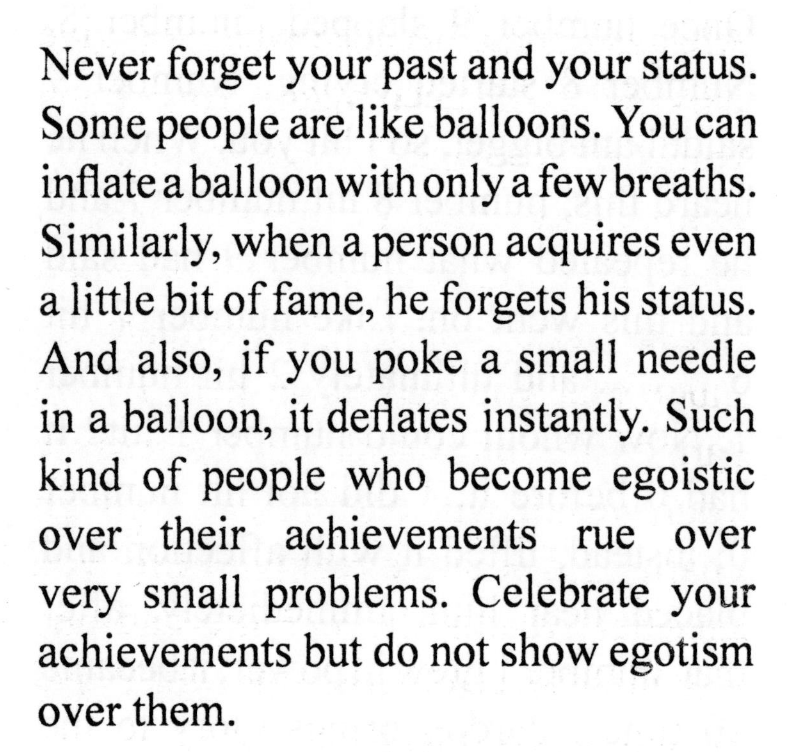

Never forget your past and your status. Some people are like balloons. You can inflate a balloon with only a few breaths. Similarly, when a person acquires even a little bit of fame, he forgets his status. And also, if you poke a small needle in a balloon, it deflates instantly. Such kind of people who become egoistic over their achievements rue over very small problems. Celebrate your achievements but do not show egotism over them.

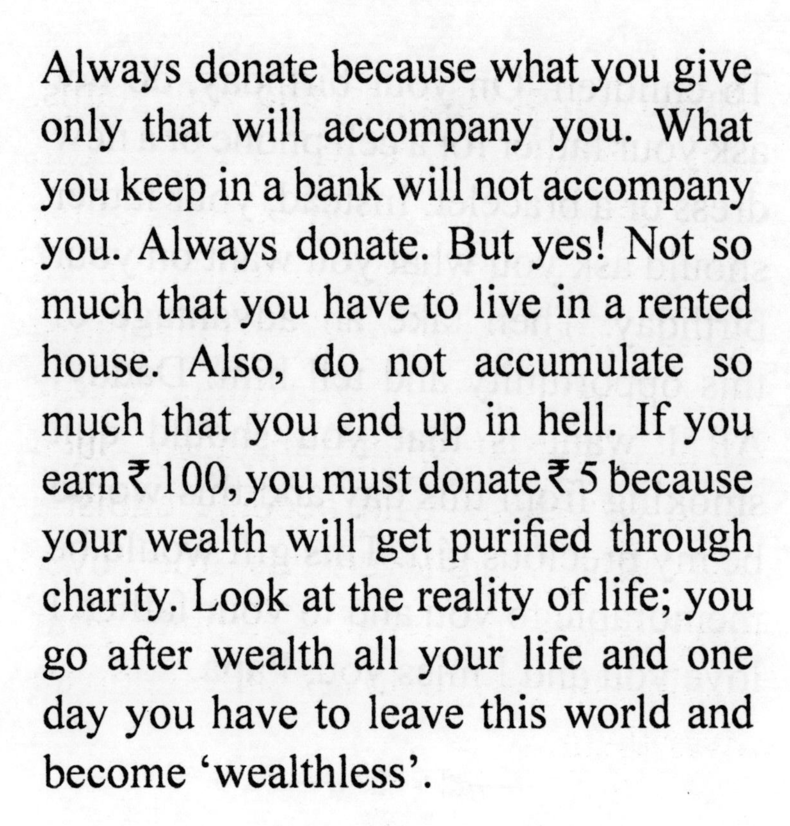

Always donate because what you give only that will accompany you. What you keep in a bank will not accompany you. Always donate. But yes! Not so much that you have to live in a rented house. Also, do not accumulate so much that you end up in hell. If you earn ₹ 100, you must donate ₹ 5 because your wealth will get purified through charity. Look at the reality of life; you go after wealth all your life and one day you have to leave this world and become 'wealthless'.

To children: On your birthday, do not ask your father for a cell phone or a new dress or a bracelet. Instead, your father should ask you what you want on your birthday. Then take an advantage of this opportunity and tell him: Daddy! All I want is that you should quit smoking from this day and this would be my precious gift. This gift would be memorable to you and to your father. I love you and I miss you, Papa.

Four thieves stole four lakh rupees. They thought of eating something and then sharing the loot. Two of them went to eat while the other two remained there to keep a watch. Those two, who had gone for food, thought to add poison in the food so that the other two might die and thus they could get ₹ 2 lakh each. The other two, who were taking care of money, thought that as soon as the other two returned, they would shoot them and thus share ₹ 2 lakh each. There, the first two added poison while the other two shot them. All of them died. The money said: Whenever I go, everybody claimed on me but I never belong to anyone.

One may experience sorrow at any time. Therefore, be ready to welcome it. Do Remember: If the good deeds arise, prosperity comes automatically without any effort and if sins arise, then whole of your prosperity vanishes in no time. When your own body is not yours then how can you claim that your wife and sons, wealth and prosperity belong to you? Therefore, be ready to leave any time, because you can't predict for any such thing which may lead you to depart from this world.

You must keep on smiling if you want to be a good human being always. Laughter is a unique gift of God. There are many ways by which anyone can smile forever like– Jokes, Cartoons, Laughter shows in T.V. and many comedians are also there to make you smile. I too want to tell you to laugh so as to make the unhappy laugh. Happiness and joy are the real possessions of life. Life is very stressful. Get off the ship of stress and board the aircraft of joy.

How the Time has changed! When you were young, you used to tell your mother to ask your father to let you go out. Now look at the situation; it is changed; even father is afraid of asking you the same. Till yeserday, this relationship of father and son was having depth but today this is just for namesake. Now, the bitter truth is that the son has taken the place of father and father has become a 'poor' father. How unluckly! My dear! This is 'Kaliyug'. Whatever is happening that's the least.